# DANNY CHUNG SUMS IT UP

by
## Maisie Chan

illustrated by
## Natelle Quek

**AMULET BOOKS · NEW YORK**

Cataloging-in-Publication Data has been applied for and may be obtained from the Library of Congress.

ISBN 978-1-4197-4821-9

Text copyright © 2021 Maisie Chan
Illustrations copyright © 2021 Natelle Quek
Book design by Marcie J. Lawrence

Originally published in the United Kingdom in 2021 by Piccadilly Press, under the title *Danny Chung Does Not Do Maths*. Published in the United States in 2021 by Amulet Books, an imprint of ABRAMS. All rights reserved. No portion of this book may be reproduced, stored in a retrieval system, or transmitted in any form or by any means, mechanical, electronic, photocopying, recording, or otherwise, without written permission from the publisher.

Printed and bound in U.S.A.
10 9 8 7 6 5 4 3 2 1

Amulet Books are available at special discounts when purchased in quantity for premiums and promotions as well as fundraising or educational use. Special editions can also be created to specification. For details, contact specialsales@abramsbooks.com or the address below.

Amulet Books® is a registered trademark of Harry N. Abrams, Inc.

**ABRAMS** The Art of Books
195 Broadway, New York, NY 10007
abramsbooks.com

This book is dedicated to the memory of Jean and Ron—
my mum and dad. And to the Chan, Kwan, and Mui families
who I grew up with and who inspired this book.

# Half Duck, Half Dragon

**Drawing makes me feel good.**

I draw literally everywhere: in bed with a flashlight, and even on the toilet (well, you can be sitting there for quite a while, and yes, I always wash my hands afterward). Sometimes I sketch in the park on weekends with Ravi, my best friend. My favorite part is coming up with new characters: ones that are half one thing and half another—the best of both worlds, like whole wheat bread and white bread put together.

I was really pleased with my newest creation, which I called a DRUCKON. It was a mutant duck with a dragon's head. It's very Chinese, if you ask me. Dragons are the most beloved and lucky creatures in Chinese mythology, and ducks are yummy and succulent. The tricky part was the head. Chinese dragons don't look like other dragons and they have no wings. Ravi is basically an expert on knights and all things medieval. He says that Chinese dragons are "anomalies," which is a nice way of saying they are weird. And they don't go around trying to eat princesses or battle knights. I think that's nice. A druckon is a Chinese win-win.

Under my duvet, I heard the door to my room squeak open.

"Danny? Where are you?" It was Ba. I could tell from the sesame-oil smell.

*Not now,* I prayed. I wasn't done drawing. I had nearly finished the camel-like head of the dragon. The duck's body would, of course, be in scale with the head. You wouldn't want a tiny duck's body and a massive dragon's head. That thing would bobble around and flop over. I slid my duvet up over my head some more, hoping Ba wouldn't see me. Saturdays were usually very busy. My parents wanted me to help out by folding menus or piling soda cans on the shelf behind the counter of our takeout restaurant downstairs. But I'd rather just draw in my pajamas instead.

"We can see you, Danny Chung," Ma's voice said. "Come on, you need to leave your bedroom now. Ba and I have to clean under your bed—it's like a garbage can under there. There has to be more space in here."

*What?* I peeked out from under the duvet. Ma was wearing her red apron, which she wore when she worked at the counter each evening, and bright yellow rubber gloves. Under her armpit was the handle of the feather duster. She was scanning my bedroom like she was on a mission. Ba knelt down with a pearly green dustpan and brush; he threw some black bags onto the carpet. Something wasn't right. His head was sweaty and he was all huffy. They never came in here to clean my room.

"Yes, we don't have much time," Ba said. "We've been so busy and now we only have a few hours left." He started frantically dragging out random things that I had shoved under my bed frame. What was going on? A few hours left until what?

Ba flung an old teddy bear out from under my bed—it only had one eye. Next, he stretched and pulled out a stack of old sketchbooks that were filled to the brim with my creations.

"Clean? But it's Saturday. Can't I just relax like the kids at school? On the weekends they play computer games and go for ice cream. Saturdays are for doing . . . I dunno . . . nothing." Uh-oh. I regretted it as soon as I had uttered the word "nothing." I was going to get my dad's Chinese Way lecture.

"Doing . . . nothing? Nothing?" Ba got up from his knees and wiped the dust bunnies and hair from his pant legs. "It is not the Chinese Way to do *nothing*, Danny." Ma raised her eyebrows at me. She knew what was coming. She started humming a little out-of-tune ditty while her feather duster skimmed the top of my wardrobe.

"The Chinese Way is hard work. It is about listening to and respecting our elders. It is about family and helping each other gain success. We have to work doubly hard in this country. Six days a week. No one gives us anything for free. We don't do . . . nothing," Ba blustered.

"I didn't mean it that way. I meant . . ." What did I mean? "I just like drawing, that's all. It's not really doing nothing. Look, I'm making something." I turned my sketchbook around so he could see what I was working on. Ma peeked over Ba's shoulder to get a glimpse and squinted, her head

4

tilted. She was obviously confused. They swapped places. Ba sighed, then got back down on the floor, and Ma moved in closer to see my picture.

"It's a dragon-and-duck hybrid," I told her. I hoped she would see how great and Chinese it was. I turned the book back toward me. They didn't get it.

"Oh okay . . . oh look, it's Blue Bear!" she said, bending down. She picked up the dirty old bear. It was more gray than blue now. "I haven't seen him for years. He just needs a good wash," Ma said, brushing off the cobwebs.

"It's kinda disgusting, Ma, and I'm eleven, not two," I said, wondering why she'd want to keep that ugly thing. "You can throw it away."

"How can you say that? Nai Nai sent it for you all the way from China," said Ma.

"She won't even know it's gone," I replied. If there was one thing I didn't mind being thrown in the trash, it was that bear. My Chinese grandmother, whom I'd never even seen, wouldn't know it had been chucked in the trash can, so why did I need to keep it?

"She *will* know, Danny . . . I mean . . . she will know that you didn't appreciate her gift," she said quickly.

Ba shook a black bag open, then grabbed a pile of my old sketchbooks.

"Ba, wait! Don't throw those away." My heart beat faster in my chest. I couldn't remember what was in those books, but I knew they deserved a better fate than the recycling bin.

He shook the dust off the top of one, then flicked through it, tutting. That wasn't a good sign. He stopped at one page entitled *DANNY CHUNG DOES NOT DO MATH.*

" 'Danny Chung does *not* do math'? What does that mean? We all do math—everybody does math." I'd forgotten I had started that particular comic strip. I'd been bored in class while Mr. Heathfield was talking about long division, and I'd begun drawing all the things I *could* be doing instead of math. That had included balancing a beach ball while playing a trumpet, blowing paper darts through a straw, and flying a giant kite in the shape of a stingray that had turbo jets.

"Oh, that was just for fun. A joke to make Ravi laugh." This was not the time to bring up how I had a hate-hate relationship with math. Often I would try to get Ravi to help me, or I would just give an excuse to Mr. Heathfield if I couldn't do something. He thought I had a dog who ate a lot of my homework.

"If you tell yourself you cannot do something, then you will not succeed at it. You need the right mindset. This . . . drawing stuff. It has no purpose." He put all of my old sketchbooks into the black bag. I felt like my hard work had been truly trashed.

"But I like it," I mumbled, hugging the book I was now working in.

Ba obviously hadn't heard about famous painters like van Gogh. (All right, he was poor during his lifetime and had a terrible incident with his ear, but now his paintings were worth millions.) I tried to think of a less tragic artist who was famous. I slid my drawings under my pillow.

"But why, Ba? Why can't I be like Picasso?"

"Why do you want to be like Pika . . . what's it . . . the yellow squeaky mouse thing from TV?" He shook his head, squinting with confusion. "That's not a career, Danny." I wondered if he was imagining, as I was, a grown-up me dressed in

7

a Pikachu onesie holding a briefcase and going to an office. I stifled a laugh.

"No, Ba. Picasso was a Spanish painter. He said, 'Every child is an artist'—he was very famous. He's not a Pokémon."

Ba sat down on the side of the bed, sliding next to me. Then he put his arm around me and gave me a squeeze.

"Son, it's for your own good that you do more constructive things with your spare time. You can draw in art class at school, but after you come home, you need to focus on getting good grades. We don't want you to be serving take-out like us when you grow up. Math, science, English—these are the subjects you have to work on."

"Your ba is right," Ma said, pulling bits of fluff from the bear.

He looked me straight in the eye. "I love you, Danny, but no more drawing, okay?"

Ba rose and glanced around the room; his brow furrowed, causing slight wrinkles in his usually smooth forehead. "Anyway, we want to make room for a new bunk bed. It's arriving in half an hour. Then I need to go and get my—" Ba was about to say something, but Ma swatted him on the arm.

She interrupted. "We need to get a move on . . . Get dressed now," she said, still clutching the blue-gray bear. "The Yees will be here any moment with the bunk bed." She glanced at Ba. It was a look that I couldn't understand.

8

"Give me some privacy and I'll get dressed, okay? I guess that's something to look forward to." I got out of bed. A new bunk bed was gonna be great because my mattress was sagging in the middle.

Ba half smiled and patted my shoulder; he looked tired. Ma led Ba out of the room with a hand on his waist. He dragged the black bag behind him like a bad Santa. *Bye, drawings! I'll miss you!* I wanted to shout. I was determined to never be in that position again. From now on I would have to do stealth drawings.

They were whispering about something while going down the stairs. I could hear Ma telling Ba off. "Not yet . . ." were the only words I could make out.

Not yet? What was *not yet*?

# CHAPTER 2

## Cyborg Devils of the House of Yee

"We come bearing gifts! Where is Danny?" Auntie Yee boomed.

Auntie Yee's voice was so loud, I could hear it upstairs as I pulled my sweatshirt over my head and zipped up my jeans. It was like she needed everyone along the main street to hear what she was saying. I flicked through my sketchbook to the comic I had done last week after Auntie Yee's visit.

I'd drawn Amelia with spiky devil horns, her mother as a robotic despot who owned a mansion full of lethal lipsticks. One turn of the lid and KABOOM! You were toast. I hadn't added any words, but I would let Ravi fill in those parts when

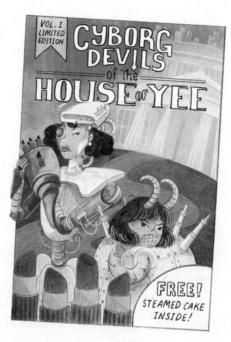

I met him at the park later. He was my comic wingman—he did the speech bubbles to my drawings. I shoved my sketchbook into my gray backpack and hopped downstairs in my slippers.

Like always, Auntie Yee looked like she had stepped out of a hair salon and a nail salon and a ladies' fashion boutique. And behind her was Auntie Yee's "mini me"—Amelia Yee. They were always in color-coordinated outfits, like weird twins. Amelia's braces glinted at me as she forced a half-smile. Being required to hang out with Amelia Yee was basically torture. She didn't want to be here—I didn't want her to be here either. But it was the Chinese Way to act respectful, and so we pretended we got along.

Auntie Yee placed a round tin on the table and opened it, revealing yet another steamed cake (if you could call it a cake), which we usually had to force down with buckets of jasmine tea.

"Hi, Auntie Yee," I said, waving. Just for the record, she wasn't my real aunt; I had to call her "auntie" because that was also the Chinese Way.

"Thank you so much for bringing the beds!" Ma said, beaming at Amelia. "You're such a kind girl."

"You know, anything to help," Amelia said, and then whispered to me under her breath so only I could hear it: "Those less fortunate." She turned to face Ma and added, "I've got a new double bed with a TV that pops up at the end. A girl at school had one and Mommy said I could have one if I passed my piano exam. I got an A-plus."

"She's excelling. Those extra lessons we bought are really doing the trick. Three times a week she has a tutor. We're so busy taking Amelia to all of her extracurricular activities. You know how it is, Su Lin!"

"Oh yes, of course . . . impressive, Amelia," Ma said. "Danny, tell Amelia about what you have been doing or your . . . things."

"My things?" I asked. I had no clue what she was talking about.

"Danny, how is school going?" Auntie Yee said. It was the question she always asked when she came. It is also the least interesting question a child could answer.

"Danny is doing well at school too," Ma interjected. "He's always working so hard. His head is always in a book." Ma patted my back and ruffled my hair. Amelia glanced at me and then smirked.

Auntie Yee was always telling my parents I should do this and that. Luckily, we just didn't have the money for fancy lessons; my parents were trying to save up to buy a new house.

"Danny, your mother told me you stopped the violin lessons. I suggest you take up the piano instead. The secret is constant practice." Auntie Yee turned to Ma. "Invest in your child and your child will invest in you when you are old, as well you know." Auntie Yee sat down.

My two months of torture last year—also known as violin lessons—were a waste of money and time. Ba was the one who begged my mom to stop paying for them. "The boy isn't talented at all—he sounds like a strangled cat," I heard him say. Ba was right; it was not my thing. In fact, I played badly on purpose! It was the one time I was glad to be awful at something.

Ba wedged open the front door of the takeaway open. I could see Uncle Yee taking long planks of white wood out of his truck and passing them to Ba to stack outside the window. Ba was looking concerned—there were a lot of parts. Uncle Yee slapped him on the back and pointed to a headboard, then carried in a whole mattress all by himself. Ba lifted up the headboard and brought it in. He was already a little breathless. Uncle Yee winked at me as he approached, the mattress in his big arms.

"Hey, little man, how are you doing?" he boomed, his bald head shining under the light. He was the only Yee I could stand.

"I'm fine, thanks," I replied.

"We'll get this beast set up in no time at all. Ready for when your— Owww." Ba accidentally nudged Uncle Yee with the headboard.

"Sorry, sorry. Couldn't see you there." Ba gave Ma an impatient look, as if to say, *Stop their chitchat.*

"Thanks so much, Adrian," Ma said. "We left you the chocolates that you like—Ferrero Rocher—on the living room coffee table; help yourself when you are up there."

"Oh, my favorite!" said Uncle Yee. He turned and bounded up the stairs with the mattress like it was made of marshmallows. Ba struggled behind with the headboard. I could hear him ricocheting off the walls as he went up.

"Come, let us sit and have some snacks," Ma said, inviting Auntie Yee and Amelia to sit at our dining table. It was behind

14

the takeaway counter and had been laid out with jasmine tea and a tin of egg rolls; a small fruit bowl sat in the middle. Auntie Yee indicated to Amelia to sit down next to her. Amelia took her furry rainbow backpack off and plonked it on the table. Everyone was trying to avoid the jaundiced sponge cake.

"Bag off the table, Amelia. We're not ruffians," said Auntie Yee. She'd been talking all "posh" since being booted out of the Women's Society, which, according to Ba, was some kind of women's club in the nearby county where they bake a lot of cakes. Her steamed Chinese sponges were not a resounding success, so she liked to bring them here. Ma sometimes told me to take them to the park to share with Ravi. We often played Frisbee with them and then scooped the pieces up and plopped them in the garbage can, as we didn't want to poison the wildlife.

Amelia grabbed her bag and shoved it to the floor near her feet. Then she got out her tablet and started to swipe left and right.

"So you are looking forward to having bunk beds, then, Danny?" asked Auntie Yee.

"Yes, I can't wait. I'm going to invite my best friend, Ravi, over for sleepovers; I'm seeing him later at the park." Ma shifted in her seat. She liked Ravi—I didn't think she would disapprove of him staying over—and in any case, she and Ba worked nearly every night, so I was alone upstairs. Ravi could keep me company and hang out. It would be great to have someone to talk to in the evenings.

"Amelia never used the top bunk—it was pointless having it to be honest. Adrian thought it would be good for sleepovers, but Amelia is too busy for those kinds of things—even weekends are full." Amelia suddenly looked strange for an instant, then took a deep breath in. I thought she was really popular at that fancy girls' school her parents paid for, but maybe she wasn't.

"I'm happy it's gone. Sleepovers are immature," Amelia chimed in. She looked up at us all for a moment, then went back to looking at her screen. Ma poured the tea.

I sat there wondering what I should do. When Uncle Yee visited, he often liked to play cards and give me his spare change. But he was busy with Ba, sorting out the bed. I picked up a sweet egg roll and started munching it. Yellow flakes fluttered onto my lap. I wiped my hands on my pants and went to slide on my sneakers, which were kept at the bottom of the stairs. Ravi would be waiting in our spot at the park, and any excuse to not listen to Auntie Yee compare me to Amelia was worth going out for. Amelia and Auntie Yee. Cyborg Devils, both of them, bashing whole villages with their handbags of destruction. Their sonic singing would shatter even the strongest windows.

"Su Lin, has Danny told you about the math competition that all of the schools in the area are entering? Amelia is sure to win," Amelia's face went bright red. "She's been working on it every weekend. While other children frivolously play in parks"—Auntie Yee looked at me—"my Amelia has been working tirelessly on her presentation." I bit my bottom lip. Our class had been nominated to represent our school in the citywide competition called Math Is Fun, too. Oh God, we didn't stand a chance against Amelia *aren't I ever so clever and good at everything* Yee. It would be one more thing for Auntie Yee to lord over my ma. Awesome. *Not.*

"Danny, you mentioned your class is also taking part, right?" said Ma. Great. Just what I didn't want Auntie Yee to know.

"Yep." I looked down, waiting for it . . .

"Yes, well, Danny, good luck, but you're up against really strong competitors from Amelia's school. You know, because it's a private school. Smaller class sizes and all that. But I'm sure your school is totally fine too." Auntie Yee picked up her tea and sipped it, her pinkie finger stuck out to the side like it was begging to be away from her. Ma picked up her mug that said KEEP CALM AND CARRY ON and gulped down some tea.

"Mommy, I want to go home. I've got a headache." Amelia gathered her tablet and jacket and put them in her bag. Ma was confused, and Auntie Yee seemed annoyed; this was their only adult social activity. Being the only two Chinese families within five miles of each other had made my mom and Auntie

Yee like magnets. They stuck together but were opposites in many ways.

"But, darling, your father is still assembling the bed," Auntie Yee called out as Amelia walked toward the front door.

"I want to go," Amelia repeated.

"Can I do anything?" Ma said. She got up, worry plastered on her face. She didn't want to upset her only friend. "Was it something you ate?" I knew that Amelia hadn't touched a thing. It was something else.

"I'm sorry, Su Lin, we'll all have to go. I'm sure you can figure the bed out yourselves." Auntie Yee trotted over to the stairs and called up, "Adrian, we have to go! Amelia has an issue. Adrian. *Now!*" Uncle Yee's feet thudded down the stairs, making our TV rattle. He appeared flustered.

"What? We need to go? But I haven't got the frame done yet," he said, munching on a Ferrero Rocher.

"I'm sure it will be fine. Danny can help. Come on now." She tugged at Uncle Yee's rolled-up sleeve. He shrugged and held his hands up in defeat.

"Sorry, Danny. I hope the bed is up for your big surprise." Uncle Yee patted me on the back. I heard Ba jogging down the stairs.

Auntie Yee had almost made it to the front door. "Amelia, darling, we are coming! Su Lin, I'll see you in a couple of weeks, and then we can go out for dim sum when the kids are off for Easter, okay? Call me." Auntie Yee yanked Uncle Yee out of the takeaway.

"What *is* this surprise, Ma?" I asked. She turned to me and put the whole steamed cake into a paper bag so I could take it to the park for a snack.

"Who will be surprised?" said Ba, joining in the conversation, sweat running down his face.

"You," she said to him. "The surprise is that we have to build the beds ourselves, because the Yees have left us to do it. We've only got two hours before you are due to get the 'surprise.'" Ma used her fingers in air quotations when she said "surprise" and raised her eyebrows at Ba.

"Why isn't anyone telling me what's going on? What is my surprise?" I repeated, bouncing up and down on my toes.

"Ahh, Danny, we don't often get you surprises, so we want to make sure it's a special occasion." Ma had tears welling up in her eyes.

Ba put his arm around my shoulders. "Danny, just go out and play in the park, okay? Be home by four and then you will see. You will love it!"

I felt butterflies in my stomach. I grinned at them both. It wasn't my birthday or Chinese New Year, and here I was getting a bunk bed *and* another surprise! They didn't have to tell me twice to scram.

## Sir Ravi of Longdale

**There wasn't much to do in my neighborhood apart from going to the park.** It was less than fifteen minutes down the main street, where our takeaway, Lucky Dragon, was. On weekends, I would meet Ravi at the bench near the playground. He was already sitting on it and reading a comic when I arrived.

"Hey! What's up?" Ravi said, wearing new bright white sneakers with a red check mark on the side. I was wearing his old black ones from a couple of years ago. I was an average-sized kid for my age, but Ravi was already wearing clothes for fourteen-year-olds. He could be a basketball player if he wanted to be, except he was terrible at catching. And throwing. And hated running.

"Your sneakers are so bright, you can probably see them from Mars," I chuckled. "Hey, guess what?" I sat down next to him and opened my backpack (another Ravi hand-me-down).

He pushed up his glasses and frowned, putting his comic on the bench. "Errr . . . Mr. Heathfield has taken the whole year off and we won't have to do that math 'thing' he's been talking about and embarrass ourselves in front of the whole class?"

"If only. That would have been nice, but no . . . you, my oldest and most esteemed friend, can now come over for . . . sleepovers!" I poked him in the ribs with my finger multiple times. It was more like a tickle poke. He jiggled out of the way.

"Stop it!" Ravi laughed. "But where would I sleep? Your room is tiny. I don't do floors. Our house might be overcrowded, but I ain't no peasant."

"This morning the Yees, instead of giving me indigestion or a headache, brought over a bunk bed! My parents are making it as we speak. My dad was a bit stressed because the Yees basically dumped it and left him to it."

"A sleepover would be amazing, just one night . . . one night away from Vishal's stinky backside. I tell you, Mom should stop giving him eggs. Every time he eats eggs . . . our bedroom smells like a trash can with a fart machine trapped inside. You're lucky you're an only child. My house is always so full of people, I can't think sometimes."

"Ah, but at least you have a game room you can escape to, and a backyard."

"Yeah, but I can't sleep there, can I?" Ravi grinned at me, hopeful.

"Our apartment's sometimes a bit boring, though. You know my parents, always working downstairs. They want me to do well at school, but they never have time to help me with my homework or play games."

"My parents don't do that either. Dad's always working and Mom's dealing with Vishal or trying to stop my sisters from failing their exams. You can do what you want at home. No one's breathing down your neck, because they're always in the kitchen."

"Well, I'm just saying, it can get a bit . . . you know . . . quiet . . . not that I'm lonely or anything."

Carter and Mitchell from our class appeared from the field next to the park and started running toward the playground, Blaster guns held across their chests. They charged over dirt-filled flower beds that had no flowers in them. Carter hit Mitchell with the navy-and-yellow foam pellets, and they weaved in and out of the hedges. Jay Jay, the smallest of their gang, stayed in the bushes. They didn't notice us, or if they did, they just ignored us.

I turned back to Ravi.

"Want some Frisbee cake?" I asked, lifting up Auntie Yee's sponge.

"No, thanks," he replied, eyeing Carter and his crew. "Do you think we should move away from them?" Ravi asked me as his foot began to tap nervously on the ground.

"I think we're okay. It's a big park and it's not like they'd ever ask us to play." Although, secretly, I'd really like to play Blaster Hide-and-Seek—Carter said he'd invented it. They talked about it all the time at school, and it looked like so much fun. But as I said, they'd never asked us, and Ravi disliked Carter, so it wasn't going to happen.

I sneaked a peek at Carter's Blaster. It was one of the automatic ones I'd seen on TV! A limited edition! The three of them even had walkie-talkies. Cool. Ravi broke my staring with a poke in the ribs. We liked to call them "finger jousts," because it sounded medieval.

"Hey. Hello? Earth calling Sir Danny."

"Sorry? What?" I didn't want to upset Ravi, but, man, I wished he'd be a bit more like the knights he loved so much—you know, running around on quests and missions. He preferred to read about them instead of acting like one.

"What shall we do now?" Ravi said.

"Do you want to do the speech bubbles for the Cyborg Devils?" I asked.

"Does a duck swim in water? Yeah, of course I do. Pass it here." Ravi held out his hand.

I opened up my sketchbook. The Cyborg Devils section took up a lot of the front of the book. Later in the comic, Amelia had morphed into a Transformer with a metal grill for a mouth and spiky diamonds of death coming out of her shoulder pads. Her mother had become a mechanical poodle mixed with a wrestler. Ravi laughed when I showed him. Then I remembered what I had drawn that morning.

"Oh, hang on . . . Look, I think you will appreciate this," I said, and opened the page to the druckon. "It's a dragon mutant duck." I handed it to Ravi. He studied the page and began nodding, chuckling to himself.

"Yeah, yeah, it's fierce. I love it. The Deadly Druckon of Longdale . . . Ohh, ohh, can I add something?" I passed him a pencil from my bag. He began to scribble in his tiny handwriting.

"Oww, what was that?" Ravi said, rubbing the back of his head and slowly turned. I could see Carter, Mitchell, and Jay Jay coming toward us. I looked at Ravi; he raised his eyebrows.

"Just when you're having fun, they show up," Ravi said. He and Carter used to be friends in preschool. But Carter had dumped him on the first day of elementary school to hang out with Jay Jay and Mitchell. Ravi had never forgotten it. Carter often ignored Ravi, like he didn't exist.

"That's mine," said a familiar voice. Carter was shorter than both Ravi and I, but his gelled-up hair made him seem big. He had a sprinkle of facial hair above his lip, and his chest was nearly double the size of ours. He was solid despite being in the same grade as us. He held his Blaster across his chest with two hands like he was a stormtrooper on a mission. Mitchell and Jay Jay were jogging behind him, grinning like hyenas.

"Is this the Knights of the Round *Loser* Table or whatever it is you two like to play?" Mitchell asked.

"Haha, yeah, remember they do that poking thing at school!" Jay Jay said, jabbing his finger into Mitchell's armpit. Mitchell was laughing his head off, trying to stab his finger into Jay Jay's side.

"It's finger jousting, idiots," Ravi mumbled under his breath.

Ravi's shoulders hunched and he closed the sketchbook that was on his lap and dropped it into my bag. They were always saying mean stuff about Ravi's love of knights. He knew it was best if they didn't see the stuff we had drawn.

"Oh, hi, Carter," I said. I bent down to pick up the pellet that had hit Ravi, and I stood up tall. "I really like your Blaster. That one's cool. I saw it on TV." And I *did* really like his blaster; I wasn't just saying that so I wouldn't get shot in the head with a foam pellet like Ravi had. I heard a small sigh from my best friend.

"Yeah, my dad bought it for me last weekend," Carter said. He was wearing khaki combat pants and had black stripes on his face. Rumor had it that Carter's dad bought him anything he wanted because he'd gotten a new family and felt guilty about leaving Carter and his mom. Mitchell and Jay Jay had Blasters and black stripes on their faces too.

"Shame your aim is so bad," said Ravi, leaning his elbows on his knees.

"I think his aim was pretty good," jeered Jay Jay.

I had a flashback to World Book Day in kindergarten, when Mitchell had thrown Ravi's knight sword onto the roof of the bike shed. I wondered if I could do anything to dampen the tension and make them go away. Carter just stood there and laughed. I really couldn't believe he and Ravi had once been friends.

"Hey, Carter, I have a rubbery cake. You can have it if you want. It can be like one of those clay pigeon things you shoot?" I grabbed my bag and handed him Auntie Yee's steamed cake. "You can throw it into the air and try to hit it."

Carter took the cake and passed it to Jay Jay, who threw it high into the sky.

"All right, later, we're out of here, geeks!" shouted Mitchell. Carter ran off, Blaster aimed to the sky, trying to hit Auntie Yee's inedible sponge. They were always calling us "geeks," but geeks were smart. And we weren't. The label just didn't fit.

"See ya, wouldn't wanna be ya!" shouted Jay Jay, jogging off. I watched as the three of them ran around trying to hit the yellow disc. It kinda looked like fun. Jay Jay and Mitchell were the ones who always said mean stuff to us, which made me think that maybe Carter wasn't so bad. But Ravi said, "Birds of a feather flock together."

"Carter thinks he's in the actual army!" I whispered. Ravi forced a laugh but was still rubbing the back of his head. "I like that Blaster he has. I wonder how much they cost," I said. "Maybe we should get some? They might let us play if we had the right stuff. If we show them that we aren't geeks?"

"Looks silly, if you ask me," Ravi grumbled.

"Yeah, probably . . . probably silly, like you said," I replied.

"There are too many wannabe soldiers around here for my liking."

I knew that when Ravi got like this, I had to change the subject fast. "Hey, can you help me come up with the words for my druckon?"

"Sure," said Ravi sullenly. *A bit of comic-creating might cheer him up,* I thought. He began to write. I glanced over as he scribbled some words.

We spent hours working on a whole story line. The druckon devoured the evil warlord's henchmen (henchmen always die in films), and the evil warlord begged for forgiveness, giving up his catapult forever. It was awesome. Ravi even said the druckon could lay eggs at the end and create an army of his own. A baby druckon army! That was why Ravi and I made a good team. He came up with some great ideas.

After we'd finished, I packed up my pencil case and sketchbook.

"Wanna come back to my place for a bit?" Ravi asked, rolling up his comic. He slid it into his inside jacket pocket.

"Can't. My dad's bringing me some kind of surprise."

"But it's not your birthday until August," Ravi said. "That's months away." He always remembered my birthday and my phone number by heart, mainly because we're the only kids in our grade who don't have cell phones yet. Tia from school calls us "retro."

"I know. I can't wait to see what it is!"

"Well, let me know at school on Monday what you get, and we can start planning the bestest, fiercest sleepover ever." Ravi stood up.

"I will. See ya, Sir Ravi," I said, jabbing him in the ribs with my index finger.

# CHAPTER 4

## THIS IS MY SURPRISE?

**The takeaway smelled like incense when I returned.** The wooden altar on the wall where my parents prayed to the kitchen god was full of offerings and lit joss sticks. The smoke wafted around the room in swirls of gray. Some large red-and-white laundry bags were leaning against the counter. I peeked inside to see if there was a cool thing for me, perhaps a Blaster or a game console, but there were only clothes in there. I heard muffled noises and footsteps in our apartment above.

I quickly took my sneakers off and galloped up.

"Ma? Ba?" I called out as I pounded up the stairs.

Ba stood in my bedroom doorway, blocking my view. Trying to peer around him wasn't working—he sidestepped, blocking me more. The plastic boxes that had always been in a corner of my room were now out on the landing.

"Wait a minute, Danny," Ba said. He was beaming.

"Hi, Danny, we're finished making your bed," said Ma, behind him. "We're so relieved it was easier than it looked."

I had a warm, squiggly feeling in my belly. The anticipation was eating me alive.

"Ah, Ba! Let me in!" I bobbed my head to one side.

"You're going to be so happy," Ma said, peeking her head under my dad's armpit. She was grinning from ear to ear. I hadn't seen her smiling like this in a long time.

"Danny, it's going to be different, and you will have to adjust, but it will be so good for you to have links to your roots now," Ba said.

Roots? What was Ba talking about? Had they done a sixty-minute makeover on my bedroom like they do on TV? I'd wanted a room makeover for ages now—some cool bean-bags, and matching duvets, maybe. I heard a cough. Someone was in my room. Was it Uncle Yee again? Had he come back to help?

"Close your eyes," Ba said. He put his warm hands over my eyes, and I edged forward like a blind zombie, one wobbly step at a time.

"It is so exciting! Come, come," said Ma. Ba moved his hands away. I blinked eagerly, searching for something that resembled a gift. The room looked exactly the same as it had that morning. The wallpaper still had ugly flowers on it; the curtains were a dull brown. I felt disappointed that the walls hadn't been painted over. Nothing seemed that different apart from the towering white bunk bed, which looked great, and a little old lady who sat on the lower bunk.

A little old lady who had the same nose as my dad.

She had gray hair fashioned into a short bob with a headband. She wore a baggy purple cardigan that had pockets that bulged as if they were full. Her feet hung precariously off the ground like a toddler's. She stood up and stepped toward me with her arms outstretched. As her mouth opened into a grin, I noticed that a couple of her top teeth were made of gold, like a pirate's, and the rest were slightly yellow.

The strange old woman scuttled forward and took hold of me around my waist. I glanced down to see her face. Her wrinkles smiled when she did.

"Why-is-she-in-my-room?" I asked, breathing heavily. I craned my neck to look at my parents. They stood holding each other's hands. What was going on? They never held hands.

"She's my mother, Danny—your nai nai. She's come to live with us." Ba came toward us. I felt like prey being squeezed by a python. Nai Nai? She was here? In Longdale?

Ba crouched down and put his arm around the stranger—I was now encased in a multiple hug. I glanced over to Ma, and her eyes were welling with tears. I felt like I could cry too, but obviously for other reasons. The old woman let me go. It slowly dawned on me why I had a bunk bed.

No . . . it *had* to be a joke.

Bunk bed.

Little old lady who looked like my dad from China?

NO WAY!

My face must have contorted into a frown, because my ba leaned toward me and said through gritted teeth: "Danny, we have to respect our elders. Give Nai Nai a hug." He pushed my back. "She has been waiting for you to get home so she could finally meet you in the flesh." He said it in his *I'm not really asking you* voice.

"She wants to hold you and tell you how much she loves you. We've been planning this big surprise for you for months," Ma added.

Nai Nai started chattering to me in sounds I didn't recognize. It only vaguely sounded like the Cantonese that my parents spoke to each other, of which I only knew a few words, like "egg" and "cat," which would not get me very far in any conversation. Of course, Amelia attended the Chinese school in the city and was already fluent in both Cantonese and Mandarin.

Nai Nai sounded like some combination of a baby singing and a frog. She took my hand and patted it with hers. The skin on her fingers was dry, but her hands were warm.

"Why's she talking like that?" I asked. She moved forward and grabbed my face. Holding both cheeks between her thumb and index fingers, she began wiggling them back and forth, pinching the fat in her fingers.

"It's Mandarin Chinese mixed with her local dialect. She lived in an area where they spoke this language. She had her own store. She's very smart," said Ba.

Nai Nai pulled me close to her again, this time resting her head on my chest, and squeezed me. There was a lot of squeezing going on. I'm not a boy who likes hugs. Maybe I could teach her to finger joust rather than doing the huggy thing?

"She's hugging me . . . too much . . ." I gasped. For someone so small, she was sure strong.

She let go and gave me a big wet kiss on the cheek. I rubbed it off with the back of my hand and wiped it on the side of my top.

"Has she always been this small, or has she shrunk?" I asked, eyeing her for size. She went over to a bag on the floor.

"Yes, she's always been small. She used to joke she was small and mighty, like an ant," said Ba.

*Ant Gran*—I could see a comic strip being formed in my mind. Half ant, half geriatric warlord. The evil Ant Gran pulling in prey, her antennae filled with poison. I watched her bending down looking for something. She rummaged around and plucked out a package; it was book-shaped.

"Nai Nai got you a present," Ma said. Nai Nai held it out to me, using her two hands like a tray.

"Look pleased, Danny," said Ba. It was easy to see he was concerned about how I was going to behave around his mother, so I politely took the gift and nodded.

Nai Nai smiled. She let go of the flat package wrapped in festive snowman paper.

"But it's not Christmas," I said.

"Just take it and smile, Danny." Ma did the *don't be ungrateful* look.

Gingerly, I picked at the sticky tape on the back. As I unwrapped it, I saw music notes and then a picture of a violin.

"She has the memory of an elephant," said Ma. "I wrote to her last year about you starting violin lessons. I hadn't had time to update her. Don't worry, we'll give it to Amelia, and Nai Nai won't notice that you don't have a violin or any musical talent." Ma was serious. Saying I had no musical talent, even though it was true, still hurt my feelings. I put the book on the lower bunk bed and noticed that my soccer duvet was there, and the old ugly bear that had been washed and dried now sat on my pillow. Its fur was sticking up like it had been electrocuted. Oh no. That meant . . .

As if reading my mind, Nai Nai trotted over to the bunk bed and began to climb the ladder. She went up halfway and pulled down a handbag. Not only would I have to share my room with her, she had taken the cooler bed. My duvet had been relegated . . . no . . . *I* had been relegated to the bottom bunk, and I'd have to sleep with that bear. And a wrinkly old lady.

"I was going to sleep up there," I half-heartedly said, knowing there was going to be little I could do about it. In Chinese culture, the older you are, the more say you have. I had the smallest voice in the family. *Woe is me,* I thought.

Ba said, "She wanted to be closer to heaven up there." His face was finally relaxed. He actually looked happy.

Nai Nai came down and searched in her handbag. She extracted a maroon-and-white-striped knit hat with a pom-pom and, as if my humiliation couldn't get any worse, she put it on my head and pulled it down over my ears. It took all of my energy not to roll my eyes. My back stiffened and my shoulders began reaching up to my ears. I felt so uncomfortable in it. It felt like a million centipedes were crawling all over my head.

"Well?" said Ma, folding up some clothes and putting them into the chest of drawers. "You don't look that excited to have met your grandmother. You always wished we had a bigger family. Now we do." She closed the drawer a little too hard.

I, Danny Chung, had to tread carefully now. I didn't want to trigger the second Chinese Way lecture of the day. "It's not what I was expecting . . . you know, as a surprise, that's all. I was really excited about Ravi coming for sleepovers, but now he can't."

"But it's your nai nai. Your flesh and blood. She was so happy to see you still had Blue Bear. I told you she would remember him."

Nai Nai gave me one more kiss on the cheek and then climbed the ladder. She pulled the duvet over her tiny body and within two minutes was snoring. Her snores sounded like a whistle. It was only four thirty in the afternoon.

"Why is she going to bed already?" I asked.

"Jet lag—she's exhausted from her trip. She'll get up for dinner," Ba said. "Come on, let's go out so she can rest."

We all tiptoed out of my bedroom and congregated in the living room, across the landing. Ma closed the door.

"Are you all right, Danny? You look . . . a bit . . . pale," she said, putting her hand on my forehead.

"I'm okay," I said, waving her hand off. "It's just . . ." I didn't know if I should tell the truth or make up something that they'd want to hear. I decided to try the truth. "Ba, I was wondering. Why is Nai Nai coming to live with us now? Why not when we get a bigger house? Then at least she could have her own room."

"Oh, Danny, saving money for our house will take a few more years and Nai Nai was all alone in China. When Ye Ye died three years ago, I wanted to bring her over to live with us, but there has been a lot of paperwork involved."

"Oh."

Ma sat on the edge of the sofa and began to stroke my hair. "We thought you would love having this surprise. Now you won't be all alone up here while we work."

"Couldn't she stay in the living room on the sofa? I don't get why she is sharing a room with me."

"It won't be forever, just a few years." Ba was looking at me like perhaps I wasn't going to be the best grandson in the world.

What would happen when I had to go to high school? Would I still be sharing a room with my gran? Imagine if everyone knew. I wanted to curl up and disintegrate into a thousand pieces at the thought.

"We've got to get back to the kitchen now. We'll have dinner together in a bit and I can translate for you. Even your ma doesn't understand everything Nai Nai says." Ba looked tired.

"Tomorrow we'll show her around. She wants to see where you go to school and wants to spend time with you," Ma said, rubbing my back. Then they left me. I was stuck. I didn't want to go downstairs and I couldn't go to my room. I turned on the TV and slumped on the sofa.

Nai Nai didn't wake up for dinner; she kept snoring into the night. The whistling snore escalated into a full *rhino charging straight at me* type of sound. Not just one rhino. A herd.

It took me forever to get to sleep that night. It got so bad that I balled up toilet paper and stuck it in my ears; then I tried to block out her noise with that itchy bobble hat she'd bought for me. My room just didn't feel right anymore.

# Mr. Potempa's Global Mini-Mart

**My eyes were cemented together as I dreamed about a witch-like creature.** She was following me along dark hallways; her bony finger was outstretched with a glob of smelly menthol stuff on it. Running was my only option. *Get away!* I shouted. *Get away!* I kicked and punched. I felt tapping on my arm.

Groggily, I opened my eyes and wiped the bits of sleep away from the corners. The bobble hat was still fitted snugly around my head, and the wads of toilet paper were still balled up in my ears. I blinked.

"Ahhhhhghhh!" I screamed. She was right in front of me! Nai Nai's whole face was covered in chalky green paste that was cracking as she grinned. The smell of Tiger Balm was making my eyes water. She was all over me like a sniffer dog.

"Ah, Dan," she said as she lowered her ear next to my nose. I was SO freaked out. I held my breath and felt my body go rigid like a surfboard. All I wanted to do was jump out of bed and make a run for it. My mouth formed a half-smile. My hand appeared from under the duvet and gave her a little wave.

She grinned back at me. She touched my forehead.

"Zao," she said with a funny drawl. She gently took off the bobble hat and used some of the tissue from my ears to wipe my brow. Then she waddled out of the room. I heard the bathroom door lock.

I sprang out of bed and grabbed some clothes from the floor and a pair of clean underwear. I would have to speed dress before she came back. Was this how I would have to get dressed from now on? I opened my bedroom door and peeked out. I could hear her making some high-pitched, out-of-tune noises.

Ba appeared on the landing in his dressing gown.

"Morning, Danny. I see my mother still likes to sing opera. Did you and Nai Nai sleep well?"

"She slept well. I didn't. It took me forever to get to sleep. She snores, you know! I had to wear that ugly bobble hat over my ears to muffle the sound."

"Haha, yes, my father said he was the only man who could sleep next to such a noise. You'll get used to it. People sleep next to train tracks, and after a while they can't hear the trains go past. It'll be like that." I doubted it very much—the Nai Nai locomotive was *loud*.

"Ba, Nai Nai was hovering over me this morning. She was by my bed, and her face . . . it was all green! She was touching my head like a nurse and then put her ear by my mouth."

My dad laughed. "She must have thought you had caught a cold and that was why you were wearing a hat in bed. She was just doing a health check."

I held up my fingers. "Seriously, she was this close to my face!"

"Ah, don't worry about it. She was checking that you were still breathing. She used to do it to me, too, when I was little."

"But I'm not a baby. I'm almost twelve, Ba."

"Yes, but she never saw you as a baby, so she's making up for lost time," Ba said jokingly.

"Weird, totally weird," I said. My ancient grandmother was performing baby health checks on me, and my dad was totally fine with that. I'd never heard of anything so absurd before.

"Don't worry. Once she's satisfied you're healthy, she'll stop doing it," Ba said. "She just loves you so much and wants to help you. It is the Chinese Way, I tell you. Grandparents look after their grandkids a lot in China. Family is the most important thing."

"I thought she was trying to kill me!" I said.

"Don't be silly. If she wanted to kill you, she would do it when you were asleep!" Ba said, laughing. Ma snickered too as she appeared on the landing next to Ba. She nudged him with her elbow.

"Don't scare him," Ma jested. "Come on, let's have breakfast and then we'll take her out for a walk." They went into their bedroom and shut the door.

I made my way down to the dining table. Nai Nai appeared with her newly washed face and sat down, pulling her chair close to mine. She poured herself some hot water from the thermos. Then poured me some. Ba appeared with Yorkshire pudding, congee, and some steamed broccoli. Nai Nai rubbed her hands together, then grabbed my cheeks and gave them a pinch.

"Mmm, yeah, fantastic," I groaned as Nai Nai began ladling congee, then more and more, into my bowl. I waved my hands over my bowl, hoping to get her to stop. "Thanks . . . er . . . no more . . . too much. Thanks." Then she gave herself about a quarter of the amount she had given to me and used her chopsticks to drop broccoli into the middle of my bowl. It bobbed there like a mini island surrounded by a white sea. I looked around. This was my family now.

"So, the plan for this morning: we'll walk around the neighborhood—Nai Nai wants to see where you go to school—and then Ma and I have to come back to work, but you can show her Mr. Potempa's store. It's good that so much is within walking distance," Ba said.

"Let's show her the park before school so she can see the daffodils before they die. Plus, it's the nicest part of Longdale," Ma said.

"They already took those out; the flower beds are empty," I said, recalling yesterday's encounter with Carter, when he was trudging through the muddy, flower-less heaps of soil.

"That's a shame," Ma said as she picked up another piece of broccoli and dropped it into my bowl. Why was everyone dropping green stuff into my bowl?

I reluctantly crunched on the steamed vegetables.

"Ba, why didn't I ever get to meet Nai Nai before yesterday?" I asked.

"Not now, Danny, just have your food," Ba said, looking down into his congee.

I held a Yorkshire pudding between my chopsticks. "But it's weird. Why can't you tell me?" Nai Nai was also munching on one but was using her hands and licking them after each bite.

Ma put her chopsticks down and looked from my dad to me. "The short version is that your ba and Ye Ye didn't always

**44**

get along. They didn't have the same ideas about things . . . or life." *That sounds familiar,* I thought.

"Why not?" I probed.

Ba huffed, then said, "Families are complicated, Danny. I didn't speak to him for a long time. But Nai Nai and I would speak on the phone once every few months and I would tell her all about you. I didn't get to talk things through with my father before he died." Ba's eyes welled up.

"And I would send her photos and a letter every so often," Ma added. "But enough of that sad stuff. We have Nai Nai here now. Eat up."

We walked Nai Nai around Longdale, one of Birmingham's remotest suburbs. There was hardly anyone around on the main street. Ma linked arms with her, and Ba strolled ahead, pointing at shop windows and talking in the same dialect as Nai Nai. The sausage-roll shop was closed. I wondered if they had sausage rolls in China. We turned the corner, strolling along Fairley Road and down past the park.

We walked her to my school, Longdale Middle School. The gates had been painted red last year. Nai Nai looked through the bars and said something to my dad.

"She's saying . . . it looks very auspicious. She thinks it looks like a welcoming place." Ba, animated now, began talking very fast to his mom. She was nodding and grinning. What were they saying?

Ma put her arms around my shoulders and started saying stuff to Nai Nai too. I couldn't catch anything. "I've just told her how happy you are there. Best in your class."

"Maaaaa," I groaned. "You don't have to do that. I'm not the best."

Nai Nai turned and hugged me tightly. She held my face and grinned at me and I did my best to smile.

"Danny, Ba and I need to head back to start the prep for tonight. Can you take Nai Nai to Mr. Potempa's? She needs some fruit to help her to be ... more ... more regular. You know what I mean, right?"

"Of course I know," I said.

"Yes, exactly. Great, we'll see you at home." Ba handed me a shopping bag and he and Ma said their goodbyes and left me to walk Nai Nai to the grocery store.

Nai Nai tried to walk very close to me, but I sped ahead and didn't say a word. We arrived at Mr. Potempa's Global Mini-Mart. Mr. Potempa was a large man with a thick gray mustache that covered the top of his lip and a beard that had grown down past his chin. Sometimes he had bits of food stuck in there. Once I pointed it out to him, and he laughed and said, "A snack for later!" He and his husband, David, were cool. David was from Mauritius and he worked "for the city," but that meant nothing to me. They lived above their shop like we did.

"Who's this you've brought with you, Danny?" Mr. Potempa asked, rising from his tattered gray swivel chair and placing his latest novel facedown on the countertop. He was always trying to tell Ma she should join the library so she could borrow books to read during the "quiet times" when no customers came in. He had a good point, but she said she was always too busy to read.

"This is my grandmother. She's just moved in with us."

"Hello, Danny's grandmother! Welcome!" Mr. Potempa said, waving his hand. Nai Nai had rushed off like a kid in a candy store. She was squeezing and smelling everything. She even held up a coconut to her ear and shook it. Next she lifted up a watermelon that was the size of a pug, turned it around, and sniffed it. Then she proceeded to bang it with her palm.

*Poum! Poum! Poum!* it went. Was she doing *knock-knock* to see if there was someone inside? She shook her head. She put it down. Then she picked up a smaller one and did the banging thing again. I wondered what kind of sound it was supposed to make for her to be satisfied with it. I looked over to Mr. Potempa and shrugged.

"I dunno what she's doing. Do you?"

"Yes, the Asian women always do that. They think they can

hear if it's ripe or not. Tell her my produce is all fresh. Very tasty. No need to slap it like a naughty baby," he chuckled.

"She needs some fruit for a special reason . . ." I did a funny wink at him. "You know, to do number . . . twos," I whispered, forgetting that Nai Nai couldn't understand English anyway.

"Oh, I see. Well, we've got some nice juicy plums in, also dried apricots on aisle three next to the prunes. It's stressful coming to live in a foreign country, never mind doing it at your grandmother's age. No offense, Danny's grandmother." I hadn't really thought about that.

"Here, give her this." Mr. Potempa passed me a metal basket, and I followed Nai Nai around the store like her servant. She filled it with two Galia melons, some satsumas and some kiwis. It was getting quite heavy. Then she ran over to a crate on the floor next to the fridges. Inside sat loads of red spiky balls on branches.

"Hao-a! Hao-a!" she exclaimed. She was touching the round red balls, running her finger over their little bumps. Then she ushered me to come over. I bent down next to her. I heard Mr. Potempa's feet on the floorboards.

"Oh, I see she likes the lychees," Mr. Potempa said.

"Yes, my mom loves them too. I don't eat them," I said. "They're too slimy for me, and I only eat green fruit."

"You're missing out, Danny."

Nai Nai held one up to her mouth. "Chi-a?" she said, looking

48

at me and then at Mr. Potempa. Being a translator was not in my job description. But I thought I would give it a try, even with my limited language skills.

"Can she try one?" I asked.

"Of course, go ahead." Mr. Potempa nodded.

"Chi, chi," I told Nai Nai, and put my hands to my lips to show her she could eat one.

"Look, Danny's grandmother, I will give you a very special offer. You can have four kilos of those for only five pounds. It is only for very special customers, you see."

"She won't understand you," I said.

Mr. Potempa skipped over to the counter and picked up a pad and pen. He scribbled something and then stood in front of Nai Nai. He showed her the numbers. She'd already peeled two lychees and was sucking on them in her mouth. One in each cheek—she looked like a hamster. A happy hamster.

"Hao-a!" Nai Nai nodded, still eating the white balls. Suddenly she held out her hand and spat two shiny black seeds into her palm. It was gross.

I felt a bit uncomfortable being out in public with her. "Ergh," I said.

"Here, put those seeds in here," said Mr. Potempa, holding out a wastepaper basket. She dropped the seeds in and wiped her hands on her cardigan. I could see spit marks on the purple wool. There was no end to the embarrassment. Nai Nai lifted a load of the lychees into the basket. It was now full. We walked over to the counter. I saw Mr. Potempa's novel—a romance this week. Sometimes it was whodunits.

Mr. Potempa twirled around a strange vegetable with spikes. "I've got an offer on limited-edition cauliflowers, too, if you are interested." It was the weirdest-looking vegetable I'd ever seen. I heaved the basket onto the counter and Nai Nai excitedly took the cauliflower thing. She was gawking at it with eyes wide. She ran her hand over the top, then held it out for me to do the same. It felt funny. I traced my fingers around its spiky turrets.

"A Romanesco cauliflower," Mr. Potempa said. "They are one of my bestsellers, but I don't have them in often." It was so out of this world. I imagined the spikes as something I could draw for a character—the back of a special turtle or something like that. That would be a fun comic.

"I don't think we can carry ALL of this home," I said.

Mr. Potempa began ringing up Nai Nai's fruit bounty. When she saw the total, she rummaged through her little pink silk purse. Then I saw her look up, calculating if she had enough. She took out the exact amount in change and moved the cauliflower back to its home on the counter, ready to entice someone else.

"Not enough cash today? Don't worry, there will be another

shipment in a few weeks," said Mr. Potempa, putting the money into the cash register. He gave me a free lollipop.

I thought it strange that Nai Nai would understand our numerical digits. I was sure the Chinese had their own way of writing down numbers. I made a mental note to ask Ma about it. Even though Nai Nai couldn't speak English, it was useful to know she could at least go shopping by herself. Then she could spit her seeds into the trash without me witnessing such things.

# ANT GRAN, SUPERVILLAIN

**I never thought I would say that I was looking forward to being at school, but today I was.** There was no way I was going to sit at breakfast with Nai Nai pinching my face and trying to feed me loads of food. How many times do you need to ask a person if they are hungry?

I got up mega early to try to make sure that I wasn't woken up by Nai Nai tapping my arm again or hovering over me with her creepy moisturizing mask. But she beat me to it. Her bed was empty. And I noticed she had placed Blue Bear next to my schoolbag. As if I would take that thing to school. I chucked it across the room, then grabbed my sketchbook and pencils. I made my way to the bathroom and locked the door. With a pencil in one hand and my toothbrush dangling from my mouth, I drew my new nemesis—Ant Gran. She was every-where. Not cool. I finished brushing my teeth. When I was done, I rushed back to my room, put on my uniform, and sprinted downstairs with my backpack. I put on my shoes so I could scram before she got hold of me.

Nai Nai was in the customer waiting area in a teal velour tracksuit. Her bare feet were tiny, her toenails painted bright red. She was punching the air and making "ha" sounds. Ma brushed past me and put a finger to her lips.

"Qigong," Ma said.

"What *gong*?" I whispered.

"She's cultivating her life force—it will help her go to the bathroom."

"Oh." As long as she wasn't planning on sucking out my life force, I would be okay. The qigong was probably working, since she wasn't like any old ladies I had seen around here—she was definitely not frail.

Ba rounded the corner; he was dressed in a new shirt and a nice sweater. Nai Nai had brought him clothes too, it seemed.

"Morning, Danny!" he said, full of smiles.

"Morning, Ba."

"It's a bit cloudy outside," Ma said, bringing out bowls. "I hope the rain stays away and I hope Nai Nai likes where we live."

"Well, it's certainly different from where I grew up," Ba replied. "It's a lot colder here, for sure. She already commented on the many pale faces. On the drive back from the airport, she was looking out the window, pointing. 'There's one. Another one. And another.' It was really funny. I told her to get used to it."

I shoved a can of soda into my backpack and wondered if I could sneak out some cereal without having to sit down to eat. Everyone was looking at me. Nai Nai finished her gong thing and came behind the counter and sat down. She said something to Ba. He turned to me. "She said she is here to look after you because you are kindred dragons."

"What do you mean, we're dragons?" I asked, trying to make my way toward the front door.

"Both born in the year of the dragon," Ba said.

"Oh right, yeah."

"You are both my lucky dragons," Ba said, smiling at me. He nodded as Nai Nai went on talking. Ba came over to me, tapped on his phone screen, and showed me the characteristics of being born in the year of the dragon:

DRAGONS ARE FIGHTERS
THEY ARE GOOD AT ART, POLITICS,
AND EDUCATION.
THEY HAVE QUICK-PACED THINKING.
THEY WORK BETTER IN A TEAM.

"See? You two will be a great team," Ba said. "Two clever, quick-thinking people . . . my lucky dragons."

Well, I was good at art. That was the only one that sounded accurate. We were definitely not good as a team. I was nothing like Nai Nai. Speaking of which, she was waving at me to sit by her. It was my cue to leave. I'd grab something from the corner shop near school.

"I've gotta go now," I said.

"What about breakfast?" Ma asked, laying out the spoons. "You don't even have your raincoat on."

"I'll grab something later—and look, it's not wet out."

"All right," Ma said. Nai Nai looked confused.

"See ya," I said, as I started to jog toward the door.

"Wait," Ba said.

"What?"

Ma opened her eyes wide and nodded to Nai Nai.

"Huh?"

"Tell her goodbye too. Don't ignore her."

"BYE BYE, Nai Nai!" I yelled.

"She's old, not deaf, Danny," Ba said.

Nai Nai raised her hand and waved. Then she waddled to the front door and watched me leave. I turned around and she was still watching and muttering something. She didn't venture out. A double-decker bus zoomed past her, and she ducked back inside. Perhaps the sounds of England were a bit much for my new little grandma from China. Fighting dragons? Yeah, right.

As I entered the school grounds, the vibe was electric. Loads of people from my class were gathered around a newly buzz-cut Carter, who was showing everyone his new cell phone. He'd given Mitchell his old one. I poked my head into the crowd to see what all the fuss was about.

"Wow, awesome app. So cool."

"Cool haircut, Carter."

"It's totally awesome . . ." Blah blah blah.

I raced over to Ravi, who was waiting for me at the bench on the far side of the playground. It was our spot. He waved to me. He was always at school early because his mom had to zoom over to the preschool to drop off his little brother, then take his sisters to the high school, where we'd both be going to in a couple of years.

"Hey, Ravi."

"Hey. You're early today."

"Yep." I wasn't sure how to broach the subject of Nai Nai.

Ravi moved his glasses up his nose. "So, what was your surprise?"

I decided to just tell him. "A Chinese granny."

"Stop being stupid. What did you really get?"

"I just told you." It did sound stupid, I had to admit.

"What do you mean? Are you talking in code?"

"My dad's mother flew all the way from China and landed in my bedroom—on the top bunk, to be precise. It's not a joke."

"No way! Are you being serious? You're sharing a room with your granny?" Ravi's eyes widened and his mouth was attempting not to smile.

"I wouldn't make up something like that," I said, scrunching up my face.

Ravi sat back against the wood. "Man, I'm sorry for your predicament. And for mine, since now I can't come and sleep over." He looked annoyed for a moment, but then he saw the bright side. "Did she bring you any presents? My nani always gets me clothes and DVDs when she comes over from India."

"She gave me a woolly hat. You know I look like a peanut head when I wear a hat of any kind. Oh, and she gave me a violin book."

"You don't play the violin."

"I know."

"Sorry, man." Ravi tilted his head in a sympathetic way. But I could see the amusement in his eyes. "Your granny . . . from China . . . Sheesh, that was not what I was expecting."

"You don't know the half of it. She follows me around, kisses me, and plonks broccoli in my congee. She left footprints on the toilet seat. I could see them."

"She stands up for number two?"

"Technically, she squats, but yeah. Plus, she snores, really loud."

"Well, now you know what it feels like for me sharing my bedroom," said Ravi.

"Nope, it's not the same. A little brother whose farts smell like boiled eggs isn't the same as an old lady who doesn't speak English sharing your bedroom." I rummaged around in my backpack. "Here, look at this." I handed him the rough sketches that I'd done in secret at home.

"I only had a few minutes before I left for school to do this in the bathroom. What do you think?" Yes, the bathroom would have to become a multipurpose room from now on.

Ravi flipped through the pages. "Ohh yeah, I like this part . . ." he said.

"What d'ya think of this? See this here? She hoards fruit until it goes rotten, then fills up her gamma-ray gun with the sludge and shoots it at people." I knew Ravi would love it, maybe even more than my last comic.

"Yeah, it's cool, intergalactic—nice. Can I do a speech bubble here?"

"Sure, go ahead," I said. He was the practical one and had a way with words.

He got out a pencil and started writing in the speech bubble. He was good at that part, and his handwriting was teeny tiny, so he didn't go over the lines. I knew if I hated what he wrote, then I could just erase it. He wrote: *I will snore you to death, puny humans.*

We chuckled. It was pretty funny.

The bell rang. We got off the bench and headed toward the rest of the class, who were lined up near the main entrance.

As usual, Ravi and I were at the back. It was the safest place to be, because Carter and his boys always pushed in at the front. Ravi and I slowed down to let them settle into a line. But Carter stood back. He looked at us.

"We'll go to the back today," he said.

"Fine," Ravi replied, stooping even more than usual.

We took our places in front of Carter, Mitchell, and Jay Jay. I was trying to put my book away, when someone grabbed it out of my hand. Mitchell.

"What's this?" He held my sketchbook in the air.

"Give it back," I said. My belly was flipping inside.

"Drawing little pictures, Chung?" He shook the book by the spine. Mitchell was always trying to do things to impress Carter. I tried to grab it back.

"Mitchell, I think you should give it back," said Ravi. His voice was cracking slightly, like his throat was made of ice that someone had just stepped on with a big boot.

"Make me."

Carter held up his phone and pointed it in my direction. He was recording. "Go on, you can fight Mitchell. If you dare—he's a yellow belt in judo," he said, smirking.

"Yeah, Mitchell, throw him!" added Jay Jay. It sounded painful.

"We don't want to fight," Ravi said, looming behind me and holding up his palms. I edged to the side, wanting to move behind Ravi. We bumped elbows.

"No, we don't," I said. "I just want my book back . . . please?"

Ravi nudged me. I turned to see Mr. Heathfield coming out of the main doors; he was heading straight toward us. *Just in the nick of time*, I thought. I looked at Carter. He was peering over his phone at me. Then he saw Mr. Heathfield.

"Go get it!" said Mitchell as he lobbed the book into the air behind us. It landed in a small puddle in the grass that edged the school. I ran over to get it.

"Danny! Get back in line!" I heard Mr. Heathfield shout. I picked up my book. I flicked through to check it wasn't too messed up. Two pages were really soaked, but the back half of the book was okay. Ant Gran was saved. Not so much the Cyborg Devils comic strip. My drawings of Amelia were all smudged. I tried to wipe the dirt off with my sleeve. When I returned to the line, Mr. Heathfield had made his way to the back and stood in front of me, arms folded in front of his chest.

"Danny, I don't like having to shout at nine in the morning."

"But, sir, I—"

"You can sit outside the staff room at lunchtime. No more trouble from you today, got it?"

"Yes, sir."

I'd never had to stay in during lunch for my behavior before. It must be Nai Nai; she'd brought bad luck with her from China. So much for being a "lucky dragon."

# CHAPTER 7

## Chicken Feet Go Viral

**Sitting at the back of math class with my sketchbook out, I started to draw a landscape.** It was full of tangled weeds. They grew high around a castle. A little figure was leaning out, calling for help from the tower. He was my age. He had my hair and he held a sign. It said SAVE ME! Ant Gran was lurking in the bushes below with an arm aloft, holding a banana ray gun.

"Danny . . . Danny! . . . Earth calling Daniel Chung."

"Huh?" Quickly shoving my sketchbook under my desk, I looked up.

"Please switch on your ears." Mr. Heathfield lifted his hands up near his ears, fingers splayed, and turned imaginary knobs. "As a reminder, these are the criteria, and here is where you should be in your progress. Your math presentation is due after

the spring break. You should already have come up with your ideas about what you want to present to the class."

"But, sir, what if my cat poops on my work before we return to school? Can I get a pass?" Carter thought he was so funny. He nudged Amy, who sat next to him.

"If anybody's pets have accidents on your homework, then you will have two projects to do next semester"

"All right, sir, I was only joking." Carter slumped down into his seat, smirking.

"So we can talk about anything to do with math?" Grace asked.

"Remember, the title for the project is 'Math Is Fun!'" Mr. Heathfield moved toward the whiteboard. "The optimal word here is 'fun.' The judges want to be entertained."

"What you gonna do?" I whispered to Tia. She had only joined the class in September from Nottingham. Whenever I tried to ask her questions to be friendly, she just told me to "stop asking so many questions." Mostly, she leaned away from me and talked to Grace in pig latin.

"I've got a brilliant idea, but I'm not going to tell you, in case you steal it." She turned away from me and lifted the cover of her exercise book so I couldn't see what she was writing.

"As a reminder, the winner from the region will get the chance to meet the mayor of Birmingham, who will offer his personal limo for you and your friends to use for the day . . . plus . . . you will receive tickets to the Knights of Old Theme Park."

I turned and saw Ravi's face light up. We'd seen the ads for that place on TV. I'd never been to a theme park before, nor even seen a limo, never mind sat in one, but I knew that I would never win the math-presentation prize, so why bother? And Auntie Yee had said Amelia had been working on hers for ages now. I didn't stand a chance.

Plus, numbers and I didn't go together. Like ice cream and cucumbers. Not that I would ever tell Ba that. I looked at the clock on the wall. Not long until lunchtime. I wondered what Ma and Ba were doing right now. Ma had mentioned she was going to try to get Nai Nai a free bus pass. It sounded pretty good, being old. You got to travel for free, you got discounts at hairdressers, and you could do stuff and get away with it (like spit out your fruit seeds). I didn't know if that was an "old" thing or a Chinese thing.

"Danny . . . Danny . . . look." Ravi was tapping my shoulder with his ruler.

"Stop it." I just wanted to get through the day as quickly as possible. I was worried that Mr. Heathfield would pick on me again.

"Sir . . . there's someone on the playground. Sir," Grace blurted out, craning her neck at an angle and rising out of her seat slightly.

"It looks like the queen, sir, but with a suntan," said Damaris.

"Eyes front and center, please, class." Mr. Heathfield was getting agitated; his face was beginning to turn red.

"No, sir . . . it's not one of us . . . It's an old"—Tia pushed her glasses up her nose to see better—"lady?"

*Please don't let it be her.*

*Please don't let it be her.*

*Please, laughing Buddha, don't let it be her.*

"It's a Chinese lady, sir." Carter giggled. I sighed. *Perfect.*

Mr. Heathfield stomped to the window. "What in the name . . ." He peered through the glass. The whole class got out of their chairs to see who was roaming around the empty playground during school hours. I rushed over to the window as well; Ravi was beside me. I jostled my way to a space at the front.

Ravi leaned over to peek outside.

"Is that her? Ant Gran?" he asked, pointing.

"Yep," I said, inching away from the glass in case she saw me. We all watched as she peered through the office windows. Then she headed toward us. She pressed her face up to the window of my classroom. She squinted, trying to get a better look. Why did our school only have one level? Why, oh why, had Ma insisted that we show Nai Nai where my school was?

What was she doing here? I was already in enough trouble today. I didn't need more. But as I said earlier, I am the unluckiest boy in the world.

She spotted me. Her face beamed a massive smile. She waved.

She started tapping on the glass and then held up a plastic bag with the Lucky Dragon logo printed on it in red. Oh no, she'd brought me food. Ba and Ma shouldn't have let her out of the apartment and into the wild. What were they thinking?

"Danny . . . do you know that lady?" Mr. Heathfield was more annoyed than usual.

"Yes . . . kinda."

"You either know her or you don't."

"Okay, I do know her, sir." It was hard to admit that I was related to her. "She's my . . . er, gran."

Mr. Heathfield opened the window slightly. It looked like he was afraid she might jump in if he opened it fully.

"Erm . . . hello, you there . . . can you please go to the office? Daniel's grandmother. Yes, you." He pointed to the main door at the other side of the quadrangle. Nai Nai grinned and nodded. She waved at me. I felt my insides flip over.

I rushed back to my chair, unsure what to do.

Mr. Heathfield closed the window and moved toward me. "Okay, you can go out and ask her what she wants. Also . . . tell her that visiting during class time is very disruptive."

"I can't, sir." I reluctantly scraped my chair along the floor and half stood up.

"You can't? Whyever not?" He frowned at me incredulously.

"I can't speak her dialect, sir." Standing now, I put my hands in my pockets. My face was burning red. "Embarrassed" was too weak a word for what I was feeling.

"She's from a small place in China. The Chinese they speak there is different, sir."

"Different? Chinese is Chinese, surely. Now go."

I shrugged. People think there is only one kind of Chinese person, but there are loads of different kinds of Chinese people with different cuisines and even different languages.

I tried to block out the rest of the class laughing and the delighted whispers of "nana's boy" that followed me out of the room. I headed to the nearby reception area.

As I opened the door, Nai Nai was already standing there in anticipation. She came inside, wrapped her arms around me, and started kissing my cheek. She held out the bag. Inside was a plastic box. I lifted the lid and saw tasty browned chicken feet. I loved them. The aroma was making my mouth water. My stomach gurgled. I pushed down the lid to block out the wonderful smells.

"No, Nai Nai, I can't eat this at school. I have school lunches. You need to go home." I wanted to shoo her away but couldn't. I'd definitely be in trouble with Ba if he heard I shoved his mother.

"Chi-a, chi, chi." She opened the lid again, urging me to eat. She held up a gnarly brown talon to my lips with metal chopsticks, which she had produced from her pocket.

Torn between devouring the food and looking like a fool, I shook my head.

"No . . . I can't eat this here." I looked toward my classroom; everyone was gawking through the window that looked out into the hallway. Mr. Heathfield was writing something on the whiteboard and not paying attention. Most of my class-mates were laughing now as Nai Nai shook the chicken's foot in my face, trying to entice me to eat it. I saw Carter filming the whole thing on his phone. Then Mitchell got out his and was pointing his finger. Great.

"Dan Dan, chi." I knew the only way to get her to leave was to take the food. I opened my mouth, and she jabbed in a suc-culent piece of chicken foot. She didn't quite get it in properly, though, and my cheek was smeared with chicken feet juice. Nai Nai pushed more talons into my mouth, then licked her fingers and wiped my cheeks with them. I munched and munched. Why wouldn't it go down faster?

*Chew faster, Danny.*

*Chew faster.*

I grabbed the box and glowered at her that she should go.

"Hao, hao." She patted my arm.

I nodded.

Nai Nai looked satisfied that her role as feeder was done. I watched her walk away. I swallowed hard.

The homeroom bell rang. As I looked out the window, the sky was ominous. Sheets of rain cascaded down; not a single sliver of blue remained. It was a fitting end to a miserable day.

Carter had sent the video to Mitchell. Mitchell had then sent it to anybody in the school with a cell phone. Great. I had gone viral for being force-fed chicken feet. In the main corridor on the way out, people kept doing flapping chicken arms at me when I walked past them. The inventive ones did the noise, too—*bock, bock, bock!* Ravi and I kept our heads down as we walked out.

"Hey, come over later to brainstorm ideas for math, okay?" Ravi said. "Gotta go—my mom's taking Vishal to his preschool karate class now." Ravi jogged off to his mom's car, which was waiting outside the gate. I could tell he was trying to take my mind off being humiliated. He was thoughtful like that.

"Oi, Chung!" a voice boomed. I turned to see Mitchell holding his coat above his head like a tent. Carter was underneath; his perfect hair remained sheltered from the rain.

"Your girlfriend has come to pick you up! She can't get enough of you!" Mitchell shouted. I was confused.

"I don't have a girlfriend." I turned back around to face the gate.

Then I saw her. *Not again,* I thought.

Nai Nai was standing on top of the red wall near the entrance gate in oversized black rain boots that looked like my mom's. How had she gotten up there? She was scouring the playground, eyes squinting, looking for me, like a first mate on a pirate ship looking out of the crow's nest. Little did she know that her being here was like making me walking a metaphorical plank. *Splash goes my street cred again,* I thought.

"Dan! Dan!" she called when she spotted me. She started to wave a huge rainbow-colored umbrella at me. She was small, but you couldn't miss her. A gust of wind made her wobble slightly.

"Excuse me . . . hello? No climbing on the walls!" said one of the teachers from the main entrance. It was Mrs. Brannan, the assistant principal. She was rushing forward and flapping her hand like she was trying to swat a fly. "Oh, it's okay, emergency over . . . it's an elderly lady! Thank god it's not one of the kindergartners!"

Nai Nai was running along the top of the wall. I ran to her. The doorway was now full of parents wondering why my grandmother was shouting my name from the top of the wall.

"Dan! Dan! Da-ni-ah!"

"Get down, Nai Nai! Please get down . . . please!" I urged.

"Who's this woman here with?" called Mrs. Brannan, trying to be heard above the din of parents picking up their children.

"She's with me! I'm sorry. She couldn't see me."

"Health and safety, Danny. Health and safety. We are not insured for relatives having accidents on school grounds." Mrs. Brannan waved her arms around like a flight attendant, in a bid to get Nai Nai to dismount the wall.

"Sorry."

**71**

Nai Nai strode with precise steps along the wall to the metal gate. She had pretty good balance, as that wall was only two bricks wide. Then she hopped down and rushed toward me to hold the umbrella over my head.

A loud, thunderous rumble in the sky had kids and their grown-ups scattering as fast as they could. Nai Nai pulled me close, forcing me to link arms with her. The height difference made it awkward for us to walk side by side.

"Look at you, little nana's boy!" shouted Jay Jay as he ran past us to get into his dad's fancy car. I lowered my head and hunched my shoulders.

Mitchell skipped by and flipped up the side of our umbrella so that Nai Nai let go and it tumbled out of her hands.

"Ah, ya!" she exclaimed, tottering off quickly to retrieve it. Perfect. Another Nai Nai display for my classmates to laugh about. Nai Nai gingerly picked up the umbrella and began pulling its spokes back into some kind of hexagonal shape. She started to chatter incessantly in her dialect. Her words were harsh; I could tell from the way she was saying them. We rushed along the pavement toward home, trying to keep dry, but the wind was blowing the rain at a slant. I didn't want her to shield me with her scrappy, wonky umbrella. I just wanted her to leave me alone.

My feet were soaking by the time we got back to the takeaway. I threw my sodden school shoes at the base of the stairs and pounded upstairs in wet socks. Ma came into my room, holding a laundry basket.

"What's wrong, Danny?" she asked as she gently closed the door.

"It's Nai Nai. She came to school TWICE today!" I said, peeling my squelching socks from my feet.

"She wanted to bring the umbrella, since you didn't take your raincoat. She thought it was monsoon weather. What happened? Why are you so wet?"

"I didn't want her to come. She should have stayed here."

"Danny, that's a bit unfair. I think you're being ungrateful."

"It was embarrassing, Ma! First she comes with chicken feet and then she comes back to walk me home. I looked like an idiot in front of everyone!"

"No need to shout . . . Shh . . . she's coming up." I heard small feet padding up the stairs. The door to my bedroom opened. Nai Nai was rubbing herself with an orange hand towel.

"She was doing a nice thing. She saw you didn't have breakfast and that you weren't wearing a coat. She was being thoughtful, Danny, unlike you," Ma declared.

I wanted to get my clothes off. My school shirt was clinging to my chest. I got up and opened my wardrobe. A stack of Nai Nai's clothes toppled down from the top shelf.

"Arghhh! And this stuff in here. It's my room! I WISH SHE WEREN'T HERE! I WISH SHE HAD NEVER COME!"

I turned around, about to go to the bathroom to get changed. Ba was standing in the doorway, a pained expression spread over his face.

# CHAPTER 8

## A Pain in the Back

**"Danny Chung! I . . . I . . ."** **Ba sputtered.** His face was red and contorted. He tried to stand upright but then leaned against the wall. Silences from Ba were worse than when he told me off. He was even too upset to do the Chinese Way lecture.

He gathered himself a little.

"Nai Nai just wanted to be there for you, that's all. She didn't get to see you for the first eleven years of your life and she wants to see as much of you as possible." Ba winced and put a hand on his back.

Ma turned to Ba and stroked his upper arm with her free hand. "Danny and Nai Nai just need some time together. That will fix it . . . Are you all right?"

"It's just my back . . . It's been a little painful for a couple of days." Ba had never hurt himself like that before. "I think it was putting together that bunk bed," he said, nodding toward the towering white bed in my room.

"Here's what we're going to do. I'll carry on doing the laundry," said Ma, picking up the clothes from my floor. "You, Danny, will help more and spend time with Nai Nai. And you," she said, looking at Ba, "you will go rest."

"It's nothing. Here, give me that laundry. See? There is nothing wronnngggg!" He took the basket from my mom's hands but then dropped it. All of my dirty clothes fell out. "Argghhhh!" Ba was slightly bent over to the right. One hand was holding his back. The other grabbed hold of the doorframe.

"What's happened to you?" Ma asked. Her face looked concerned. "You can't stand up correctly." She gathered the clothes and put them back into the basket.

"She's right, Ba. Do you need to go to the hospital?" I was worried that my ungratefulness had caused Ba to go into spasms or something. However, I was also happy that he was distracted from what a terrible grandson I had been.

"I'm not going anywhere. I'm not finished with you." He turned to go back downstairs, but one of his legs buckled.

"Ouch," I said.

"Ahrghhh!" he screamed. He held his back much tighter this time. He couldn't contain how much pain he was in any longer.

"That's it. You go lie in bed. I'll sort it out," Ma said, ushering Ba into their bedroom. I heard the relief that came from lying down. Ma reappeared a few moments later. "I will do the cooking instead of your ba, and you and Nai Nai can help take the orders. It will only be for a very short time. It's always quiet early in the week," Ma said, holding my shoulder. I felt my stomach lurch. I wasn't very good at this kind of thing. Obviously, I'd seen Ma serving customers thousands of times, but I had never done it myself. And how was Nai Nai going to help? I felt my legs buckle just like Ba. What if I got the totals wrong? What if I gave people the wrong change? My head was full of math symbols clanging into one another.

Nai Nai had mysteriously changed into a tracksuit and slippers. Ma explained what had happened to Ba, and Nai Nai produced a tiny pot of Tiger Balm and headed into my parents' room. Ma went after her.

"But, Ma, I don't think I . . ." I followed her to my parents' bedroom, where Ba was groaning as Nai Nai turned him over and started rubbing the menthol-smelling goo onto his back. Ma was pulling off his slippers in a very rough manner.

"You can do it, Danny. It's just finding the number on the menu, writing it down, and adding up the total." Adding up? I can add, but I don't know about doing it under pressure.

"Arghhhh! I'll be all right in a minute!" shouted Ba as Nai Nai touched a part of his back that seemed to be really sore.

Ba tried to sit upright, but Nai Nai pushed him back down. She was doing some kind of massage on him now.

"Ma, I kinda have this math thing I need to start . . . I was hoping to go over to Ravi's place to start it . . ." I knew she wasn't listening to me. Ba's groans were drowning out my already quiet voice.

"You lie down or you'll never get better!" Ma said sternly, pointing to Ba. Then she turned to me. "We can handle it, right, Danny? The Chungs have got this! Team Chung! I don't want to waste the food we've already prepared. But maybe . . . I can get Adrian to help out later?" She grabbed her phone. I knew she was texting Auntie Yee to find out. Uncle Yee had been in the catering business for a long time and was semi-retired.

I reluctantly nodded. The math brainstorming session with Ravi would have to wait. Instead I would have to hang out with Nai Nai . . . again. Ma walked out, leaving me and Nai Nai to nurse Ba.

Ba turned his face toward me. "Your nai nai, she's very quick with numbers. Her mind sees the numbers like a human calculator. She can . . . arghhh . . . help . . . Danny . . . with the money. Lucky dragons, I told you."

Nai Nai was warbling as she rubbed his back—this was a Tiger Balm moment. I think she was enjoying looking after Ba as well.

"She was a high school math champion," said Ba. "And when I was growing up, she used to love finding out about all different kinds of math, not just addition . . . Arghhh . . . Ma! She was the practical one in our family . . ." My dad looked funny. Like he was remembering something.

Nai Nai laughed and carried on rubbing in the ointment. He talked to her and she nodded. "Hao, hao," Nai Nai said.

"Danny, I know it's not easy having her here . . . but she is so happy to see you. Can you please make a little effort? Please? Just for me?"

I felt bad for saying the horrible thing about not wanting her here. Ba was happy to see his mom and now he was in pain. I guess I could try.

Ma peered around the bedroom door.

"Okay," said Ma, "Clarissa told me that Adrian can come and help out tonight, but not until after eight, and maybe tomorrow. But I still need you and Nai Nai to man the counter for a few hours. It's good she's here. Otherwise, we'd be really stuck."

Nai Nai hopped off the bed and held her hands up. The menthol smell filled the room.

I went to the living room to call Ravi and let him know I couldn't come over. I was working with Ant Gran.

# CHAPTER 9

## Ant Gran Makes a Friend

**I stood up tall, waiting for the first customer to come in.** The pen in my hand nervously tapped the white order pad. It had a number in red at the bottom, which was ripped off and given to the customer so when it was called from the kitchen, they knew their food was ready. My stomach felt like it could flip over at any second. Nai Nai was firmly planted at the table by the TV with a mound of fruit in front of her.

"You don't need to be waiting like a meerkat for the customers, Danny," said Ma. "Sit down, watch TV. When they come in, then you can stand up. Nai Nai is here to keep you company. Remember to smile."

"All right, Ma, I'll try my best."

I looked over at the table. Nai Nai was sucking on a half-eaten plum; the juice ran down her chin. She wiped it clean with a napkin. She was watching someone dancing on TV and was obviously enjoying it. It was a show where men dressed up as women, very glamorous women.

The front door opened and an older lady came in. I'd seen her in here before, but I'd never talked to her. I hoped she was going to be nice.

"Ohh, I love that show. Gorgeous men dressed as gorgeous women. We never saw much of that when I was a wee lass."

"My mother-in-law has never seen anything like that before; she can't stop watching it," said Ma, standing by the kitchen door. "Hi, Mrs. Cruikshanks!"

"Hello, Su," the customer said, the whiskers on her chin bobbing up and down as she chuckled. I wondered how many other customers called my mom Su instead of Su Lin.

"This is my son, Danny. He'll take your order. I've got to cook tonight."

"Oh, I hope nothing's wrong with your other half?"

"He's upstairs. Bad back. He'll be okay in a couple of days. Danny, take care of Mrs. Cruikshanks. She is a regular." Ma quickly turned and disappeared. It smelled like she might be burning something.

"Okay, young man?" said Mrs. Cruikshanks. She had a long beige coat. The cuffs were dirty around the edges. She rested her arms on the counter.

"Yes. I'm fine." I didn't feel fine, though. My hands were shaking.

"So, I usually have the same thing every week. Fries, chicken chow mein. Sweet and sour pork if it's my birthday!"

"Okay."

"Is that yer wee nanny, then?"

"Yes, she's my nai nai. She arrived a couple of days ago."

"Hello, love!" Mrs. Cruikshanks started waving at Nai Nai.

Nai Nai got up and wiped her hands on a dish towel hanging over the back of her chair. She approached the counter and stood on two trays of Coke cans so she was the same height as Mrs. Cruikshanks.

"Hell-oh," Nai Nai said. It was a pretty good attempt at "hello." Nai Nai seemed happy someone was taking an interest in her.

"You been enjoying living here? It's been wetter than a week in Glasgow. Global warming, I think, although there are some down at bingo who swear it's all a conspiracy," said Mrs. Cruikshanks. "Ohh, what's that you're drawing?" I had doodled on the order pad without thinking about it.

"Oh, that? It's a cat on stilts," I replied. "Do you like playing bingo?"

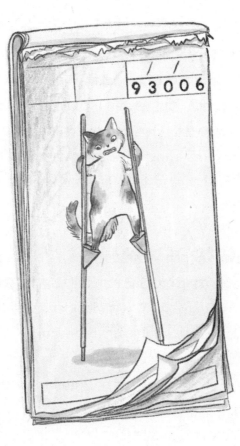

"Your drawing is fab. Yes, I love bingo. Last week I won a bottle of eau de parfum by some girl band or something. It stank to high heaven, so I gave it to Goodwill. But you can win some great stuff—vouchers, chocolate . . . which is how I lost all my teeth." I looked at her smile. She seemed to have a full mouth of perfect white teeth. I was confused.

"I haven't seen a bingo hall around here. Where do you play?" I asked.

"It's at the Longdale Community Center around the corner from the park. They have bingo every day at two p.m. Then one Saturday a month is the Grand Bingo Tournament. I've never won it myself, mind, but we can only hope. Your gran should try it. There's over-sixty yoga, too, but there's no way I'mma do that; I'd end up in the hospital . . ." I imagined her trying to get her legs around her head; it was a funny image. I'd have to try to draw that later.

"Do you know what food you want to order?" I asked, feeling very grown-up, pen at the ready.

"Yes. No . . . hang on." She was still scanning the menu on the counter. Her fingernails were long and slightly yellow as they went down each column on the menu.

"Shall I be adventurous? No . . . I'll have my usual, fries and chicken chow mein today. Number ninety-two and sixty-seven."

I wrote down the numbers and the price of each item.

"Wait! I'll have some prawn crackers and a can of Coke, too," she said. I added the amounts to the notepad.

Nai Nai was right beside me, smiling at Mrs. Cruikshanks and glancing at the order pad. It made me nervous and I couldn't think straight. I scanned under the counter to see if I could find the calculator. Our register was a relic. It didn't add up when you pushed the numbers and only one button worked that opened the cash drawer.

"Ma! I can't find the calculator!" I shouted as I rummaged around.

"I'm too busy frying; just add it up on the notepad!" Ma shouted back. I felt my palms getting sweaty.

"How much do I owe you, young man?" Mrs. Cruikshanks asked, tapping her fingers on the counter.

"Sorry . . . hang on." I bit the side of my mouth. My brain was turning to mush. I started twisting the pen cap. My neck was beginning to feel hot.

Nai Nai leaned over gently and I slid the pad toward her, giving her a hopeful look. Ba said she was a math champion, after all. She took the pen from me and, in a few seconds, wrote down the total. It was like *zap zap zap* and she knew the answer. She didn't even write down the parts you carry over. She was fast! She slid the notepad back to me. I breathed a sigh of relief.

"That's twelve pounds twenty-five please." For once, I was glad Nai Nai was here to do the calculations so fast.

"Here you go, young man." Mrs. Cruikshanks gave me the money and Nai Nai opened the cash register and gave Mrs. Cruikshanks her change.

Ripping off the order, I took it into the kitchen to Ma. I eyed the sharp spike where Ma would impale the order slip once it had been cooked. I kept my distance; the kitchen was full of loads of things that looked like they could cause major damage.

"Are you doing okay out there?" said Ma, turning to look at me quickly. The flame on the stove was huge as she poured some oil and swirled it around the wok a few times. The clanking noise of the wok hitting the burner was loud. She switched on the overhead industrial fan.

"Yes, Nai Nai is quick at math, isn't she?" I yelled.

Ma shouted back, trying to be heard over the fan. "You're doing great, Danny!" She smiled at me as she threw some chopped onions into the wok, then dashed in some vegetables and pieces of chicken.

"Thanks."

I went back to the counter. Nai Nai had walked out to the customer area and was sitting with Mrs. Cruikshanks and offering her some lychees.

"Oh, what in the name of our Lord are those slimy little things?"

"Lychees," I said.

"Leeches?"

"No, lychees. They're from China. My mom says Nai Nai loves them because they remind her of home. They grow in her province."

Nai Nai was babbling away and Mrs. Cruikshanks couldn't really understand but was smiling and nodding. They looked like old friends.

"Well, I've never tried anything like this eyeball-looking thing before. But I'll take it and give it a go. Your granny is fab. She's got such a kind face. I don't understand a word she's saying, mind, but I know a good 'un when I see one."

Ma brought out the bag with the containers in it, put it on the counter, and popped in a can of Coke from the pack Nai Nai had been standing on earlier.

"Here you go. Enjoy!" Ma wiped a bead of sweat from her brow, then disappeared back into the kitchen. Nai Nai got up and waddled to the counter area. She picked up an orange and put it into Mrs. Cruikshanks's takeaway bag.

"Thanks, love. Hey, you should come to bingo. I'm there most afternoons."

Nai Nai didn't know what had been said, so I stepped in.

"Yeah, that sounds like a good idea. I'll tell her about it."

"Good lad. See you, love!" she said as she picked up her food and left.

Phew! We did it! Nai Nai and I had served our first customer and it wasn't that terrible. I felt happy we had gotten the first one over with. Mrs. Cruikshanks was really friendly. I didn't know why I had been so worried.

Next a couple of young people came in—a man and a woman—I think older than Ravi's sisters, but not "old" like my parents.

"Hello, how can we help you?" I said, smiling at them like Ma had told me to. Nai Nai was standing next to me, ready with the pad and pen.

"We'll have two prawn and black bean sauce, one egg-fried rice, one boiled. Crab-and-sweet-corn soup and a portion of apple fritters," the woman said really fast.

I pointed to all of the items the lady had mentioned. Nai Nai jotted them down in double time and in a flash had added up the total.

"Fifteen pounds and eighty-nine pence please," I said, looking over at the pad.

"Do you take cards?" the lady asked. The man went to sit down and was using his phone.

"We do contactless—just touch it here," I said, holding up the card reader. "Thanks, it'll be about ten minutes." I took the order into the kitchen. When I came back, two more people had arrived. Nai Nai was smiling at them and nodding. The one she was serving was pointing at the numbers and she was writing down the amounts.

Two and a half hours flew by. We had a rush of people ordering, but it was easing off. And we'd been quiet for a while. Ma came out from the kitchen and slumped into a chair. I could tell her feet were aching from standing up all the time. I don't know how Ba did it every day.

"You two have been great. I'm shattered, cooking in there. It's so hot." She poured herself a mug of cooled boiled water from the flask and picked up an apple to eat.

Nai Nai and I sat down too, but I kept looking at the door, ready to spring up in case a customer came in.

Nai Nai said something to Ma, then picked up a peach and bit into it.

"Shuxue," Nai Nai said to me. Ma smiled.

"Ma, what's *shoe share*?" I asked. "Nai Nai has said it a few times tonight."

"Oh, *shuxue* means 'math.' She can help you with your calculations if you like, and maybe you can do the adding up yourself one day. Although, we have a perfectly good calculator somewhere. I wonder if your ba left it in his car. I must get the register fixed, but all these things cost money."

"And how come she understands our numbers? Don't Chinese people use symbols?" I knew that one, two, and three were just vertical lines in Chinese.

"In China they understand numerals, too. It's a universal language," she said. "I better get back to the kitchen. I hope your ba's back heals soon; I don't want you working in here too much."

The door opened wide and, instead of a customer, it was Auntie and Uncle Yee.

"Panic over! We are here!" Auntie Yee had on flat shoes and black slacks, and her hair was tied back. She was holding on to a designer shoulder bag, and in her other hand she had a pair of yellow rubber gloves. Ma smiled as Auntie Yee slid them on.

"Adrian, you cook. I can keep Su Lin company at the counter. We have come to save the day. Yet again."

Uncle Yee shook his head slightly. He came up to me and, like always, gave me a fist bump. "Hi, little man. I heard your dad hurt his back?"

"Yeah, he's upstairs in bed."

"I'll go and check on him," said Uncle Yee. He took off his sneakers and bounded upstairs. I was relieved he was here.

"Amelia is at home in her room working on her homework—that math project I mentioned. We've got the nanny cam on so we can see her," said Auntie Yee, tapping her phone. I was thankful I didn't have to put up with Amelia AND Auntie Yee.

"This must be your nai nai." Auntie Yee said something to Nai Nai, and Nai Nai mainly nodded and then babbled a few words back.

Uncle Yee appeared from the stairs carrying some empty mugs. He put on Ba's red apron and tied it tight. "Right, I'm ready to get cooking! Good job, Danny, for helping your mom.

You and your nai nai can go rest now. We've got your back." He gave me a high five.

Auntie Yee took off her shoes and the rubber gloves and sat down. "Adrian, before you begin, make me a ginger and lemon tea?"

"Certainly, Your Majesty," he said, mock bowing to her.

"Thanks, Danny. You and Nai Nai helped a lot. Go to bed now—school in the morning," Ma said.

Ma took Uncle Yee into the kitchen and I heard the kettle being put on.

Nai Nai and I were happy to head upstairs, out of the way of Auntie Yee, who had already turned off the TV. It was just past nine, and I was so tired, having not slept well for the past few days. I would work on my math project another time. I hoped Ba's back would get better soon.

# CHAPTER 10

## Blank Brain Syndrome

**Thank the laughing buddha, it was Friday.** Finally! I had been struggling all week trying to stay awake at school. Nai Nai and I had helped on the counter nearly every evening until Uncle Yee could come to take over from Ma in the kitchen. Ba had slowly been improving and could at least hobble around now. Last night he did a short stint behind the counter and was happy to be on his feet again.

Before I left for school, I quickly sketched a rhino who had a candle instead of a horn. He was going around lighting stuff, making wishes, and running away from animals who were trying to blow out his nose candle. I was having so much fun with it that I forgot the time and had to run to school. The bell had already rung when I got to the playground. I'd missed lining up.

I ran to class and saw Ravi sitting in my chair next to Tia. They were laughing about something. Ravi saw me and did a little wave, then went to his seat. Tia turned around and said something to Mitchell, who then got out his phone and began typing something.

"You look tired," said Tia, with a funny look on her face. "Anything or anyone keeping you awake at night?"

"Yeah, I'm totally wiped out." Something felt off. Tia asking me a question was weird. I turned behind me to speak to Ravi. He looked a bit pale, like he was coming down with a cold.

"Hey, Sir Ravi, did you come up with any ideas for the math project?"

"Yeah, I think so. I'm doing hip-hop fractions. My cousin Deep is going to help me with the turntables. Do you need help?"

"Yours sounds cool. I need a miracle. Are you free to meet up during spring break to help me out?"

"I'm free Tuesday, I think. Monday, my aunts and uncles are coming over for lunch . . . shhhh. Quick, turn around,

**93**

Mr. Heathfield is here." I turned to the front of the class just in time.

Giggles and whispers began to erupt all over the classroom.

"Settle down, please," said Mr. Heathfield.

I couldn't help it. I did a massive yawn.

"Late night, Mr. Chung? Or am I boring you?"

"Yes, sir, I mean no. Not boring, sir."

Mitchell put his hand up.

"Yes, Mitchell?"

"Danny's tired because he shares a bunk bed with his nana!" Mitchell blurted out.

"And she farts in the night, sir!" added Jay Jay. The whole class erupted with laughter. My face burned red-hot. I slunk farther down into my seat. I wanted the earth to open and gobble me whole. It made sense now. Tia asking me why I looked tired. Mitchell texting. That was what they were all laughing about earlier. How could they know? Who'd told them?

"The sleeping arrangements of your classmates are of no concern to you," said Mr. Heathfield. He came over to me and said gently, "Mr. Chung, head to the office. I've forgotten the attendance sheet. You can pick someone to go with you." I scanned the room. I pointed to Ravi, who slowly got up out of his seat.

I bolted out of my chair, not looking back. I felt Ravi looming behind me. Mr. Heathfield was doing me a favor; I needed to be out of that room. Everyone knew about Nai Nai in my bedroom. It was the worst of the worst. I would never live it down.

"Hey, Danny . . . wait up . . ." Ravi poked me in the side.

"Not now, Ravi," I huffed. My fists bunched tight.

"You all right?"

"Do I look all right?" I said. "It's literally the worst day at school ever. I can't think of a math project; my brain is blank right now. AND I'm trending as idiot of the whole class, maybe the whole school. I just feel like my head is full of fog 'cause I'm so tired."

"I'm sorry," said Ravi. He picked up the attendance sheet from the office table and we walked along the corridor.

"I just don't get it. How did they know about the bunk beds?" I wondered aloud. "The bus stops outside our takeaway and some people can see into my bedroom. Do you think that was it?"

"Maybe," Ravi shrugged.

"I'm worried because I'm so behind on the math project. What with all of the counter work I've been doing with Nai Nai. But my dad's back is nearly better now; he's going to work tonight. I'm so glad it's almost spring break, since school sucks right now. Hopefully by the time we come back, everyone will have forgotten all about Nai Nai and be on to the next thing they find funny."

"Yeah, I'm looking forward to it too."

I kept my head down for the rest of the day. I couldn't wait to get out of there.

As I left the school gate, I heard someone behind me. Ravi was coming toward me. "Danny, wait a minute, I have to tell you—" But then suddenly Carter was by my side.

"Hey, Danny." Was Carter going to rub it in more?

"Don't worry . . . It's nothing." Ravi waved and ran down the road to his mom's car.

"Hi," I said to Carter, nervously.

"Erm . . . that rubbery cake thing you gave me to shoot at the other day—it was pretty funny trying to hit it. I was wondering if you wanted to hang out at the park next week. I have a spare Blaster gun, and if you have any more of those cake discs we can shoot at? I'll tell the boys to behave okay. I know they can be a bit . . ."

"Oh . . . yeah, don't worry about it . . . That would be great. What day?" I didn't want to seem too eager, but I was bursting inside! Ravi and I had NEVER been invited to play with Carter and his gang, and the best thing was that I was getting a chance to play with the Blaster guns.

"How about Tuesday at two?"

"Definitely. It's on." Why did I say "it's on?" That didn't sound cool at all.

"Cool. See you near the bandstand at two, then. Oh, and come alone. I only have one extra gun." I knew what he meant: don't bring Ravi. "And, well . . . I thought you should know. It was Ravi who spilled the beans about you sharing a bunk bed with your nan."

I felt my stomach lurch.

"Oh, I didn't know that." How could my best friend do that?

"Yeah, well, maybe he's not who you think he is. See you on Tuesday, then."

"Yeah, totally, I'll definitely be there . . . by myself. Thanks, Carter." I was feeling all over the place. I was happy I was going to play Blasters with Carter, but why had Ravi told everyone about my nai nai?

When I got in, my parents and Nai Nai were sitting at the dining table, shelling prawns together.

Nai Nai held up one with its face still attached and wiggled it around. "Dan Dan, hell-oh." I almost grinned.

"How was your day? Are you all right?" Ba asked.

"I'm okay, glad school's finished."

"Danny, I'm back in the kitchen tonight," Ba said. "To thank you for helping out, we've decided you have all next week off with no chores, and as an extra treat, we'll give you spending money for snacks and ticket costs. You'll be able to do fun stuff with Nai Nai every day. You can take her to the park, find her some activities, and maybe she will make some friends."

"But . . ." I began.

"No buts," Ma said. "Otherwise, she's just around the apartment, and your ba and I have to work as usual. She's so excited to spend quality time with you." Ma and Ba, double-team, back together again.

"Yes, she worked really hard too," Ba added. "So we want her to enjoy herself . . . with you. She's super excited."

My heart dropped. I had to GRANNYSIT Nai Nai every day?

"I'm busy. I've got things going on with my friends and I have an important math project due after Easter. Can't one of you take her out?"

"No arguing, Danny," Ma said. "You will look after Nai Nai and find her lots of nice activities to do. She said she is up for anything. And you get along so well now after working together—you can bond even further. Anyway, it's not all of spring break. You, Nai Nai, and I are having dim sum with Clarissa and Amelia on Monday, at lunchtime. That will be fun," Ma added.

I took a deep breath in and looked at Nai Nai, who was now talking to a naked prawn, and sighed. Why me?

# CHAPTER 11

## DIM SUM LOVE!

**After forty-five minutes of me wedged between Nai Nai and Amelia Yee in Auntie Yee's car, we finally arrived at Tai Wu in Birmingham's Chinatown.** I often thought that the only reason my mom hung out with Auntie Yee was because she sometimes drove her places, since Ma couldn't drive and Ba was always using the van for trips to the wholesalers. Ba and Uncle Yee had declined the customary school-holiday dim sum meetup. Ma had been looking forward to taking Nai Nai out for a lovely meal. We walked from the parking lot to the entrance. The automatic doors zoomed open and my head was full of Cantopop and the smell of wonderful fried and steamed food.

Nai Nai rushed to the fish tank and indicated for me and Amelia to join her. I went over, but Amelia followed our moms and the waiter to a big round table. Nai Nai tapped the glass, trying to wake up a fish who seemed to be sleeping. A sign on the front of the tank said: "Please Watch Your Child: Do Not Tap the Glass." A big-eyed black fish came to the side of the glass. Nai Nai moved to the side and then went back to the front and put her face right up to the glass and started making a fish mouth. It was really funny.

"Danny! Over here," Ma said. Amelia and Auntie Yee were watching as Nai Nai and I made our way over to the table.

The place was filled with other Chinese people, which pleased Nai Nai. She looked around and grinned. Ma always said, "You know a Chinese restaurant is good if there are lots of Chinese people eating in there." I wondered if Nai Nai could somehow make some friends here, but it didn't look like the sort of place you could just go up to someone and ask them to be your friend.

In the middle of the table was a glass disc the size of a manhole. I spun it around.

"Not now, Danny," Ma whispered, when she saw Auntie Yee glaring at me. Nai Nai pointed at the wall. It had a massive scroll painting featuring a phoenix and a curving dragon with huge claws. I wished I had my sketchbook and pencils here. I made a mental note to draw a phoenix-type creature in my

next comic. Nai Nai passed me a pen and a paper napkin. I smiled, then drew a phoenix with a robotic fish tail eating a bowl of rice.

"Ah, they are coming around to take our order," Auntie Yee said. She spoke to the bored-looking waitress in Cantonese, never once asking Ma or Nai Nai what they wanted to eat.

A different waiter came over and placed a large black teapot in the middle of the table and five small teacups without handles, which he flipped upright, one in front of each of us. He poured tea into all of the cups. Nai Nai picked up her chopsticks and then started washing them in her teacup.

"Why's your grandmother doing that?" Amelia asked me.

"I dunno," I replied.

"Because in some parts of China, the water isn't always clean, so you wash your chopsticks in hot tea to kill germs. Sometimes when you eat out, you would do that," Ma said.

"Don't they have dishwashers?" asked Amelia.

Auntie Yee faced me and said, "Where your grandmother is from . . . it's, well, a little backward. They don't have modern appliances like washing machines and dishwashers. We're so lucky here in the West. So civilized."

"It's a little different, Clarissa; I wouldn't say *backward*." Ma looked visibly annoyed. "My mother-in-law has just arrived, so she's got to get used to things here." Ma's face went red. I felt like I could burst too. I was sick of Auntie Yee's little digs at our family. She didn't do it so much when Ba was around. Nai Nai dried her chopsticks on her cloth napkin and placed them neatly in two lines leaning on the ceramic pillow.

Puffing out my chest, I replied, "You can never be too careful," and I dunked the ends of my chopsticks in my tea just like Nai Nai had done. Then Ma did the same and smiled at me.

Nai Nai grinned and nodded. "Hao-a, hao-a."

"Amelia, sit on your chair straight," said Auntie Yee. "Why don't you show Danny your new blog post site on your tablet?"

Amelia huffed, then took out a tablet with a furry pink leopard-print cover. She swiped and tapped. She held it up in front of my face and rolled her eyes. I could tell she'd rather play games on the tablet so she could ignore me.

"Danny is doing very well," said Ma. "Nai Nai got him a violin music book."

"Oh? I thought he stopped going to lessons—isn't that what you told me?" said Auntie Yee, raising her eyebrows.

I didn't want to embarrass Ma, so I made something up. "I'm just taking a break from the violin, weighing my musical options. I'll get back to it one day," I said. I'd been happy that Nai Nai hadn't asked to see me play the violin since she'd arrived.

"Oh, that sounds like an achievement. Amelia is on grade three of the piano now. Amelia, show Danny your piano video." Auntie Yee began clicking her fingers at her daughter. I'm glad my mom didn't click her fingers at me. Amelia threw her head back and then started swiping and tapping some more. She flashed the tablet at me and then muttered under her breath: "Anything else while we're at it?"

Perfect Amelia didn't like being her mother's minion after all? I wondered if she was glued to technology because she was tired of hearing her mother's voice harping on about how good she was at everything. Imagine having to live up to that standard. I would have exploded by now. I was grateful for the parents I had—that was for sure. Amelia's finger started to slide around he screen. I noticed she had a drawing app. She held up the screen to show me.

It had the words: *OMG! THIS IS SOOOO BORING!*

I nodded in agreement. The droning on about school during the school break was definitely boring. The food would be yummy, though. I loved dim sum more than any other type of meal.

"Have you been to Knights of Old before?" I asked Amelia, now that her guard was down. Perhaps for once I would get an answer rather than a grunt.

"No, haven't been yet."

"It'd be cool to win the tickets, though. I haven't even started my project yet," I said, looking for sympathy and maybe some tips.

"Oh, Danny, I don't know if you should bother entering," Auntie Yee said. "Amelia's teacher said she has a very good chance of winning. So, we'll see."

Amelia groaned and rested her head on the table. She was busy looking at her tablet on her lap.

"How is your nai nai settling in, Danny? You must be so close." Auntie Yee was having a laugh; she knew we had to share that bunk bed.

"She is doing fine," said Ma. "Danny is very happy to spend a lot of time with his grandmother. They are making up for the many years apart. They are inseparable—they love each other so much." Ma nodded at me like she was urging me to agree.

"Inseparable," I said.

"How wonderful, the younger generation taking an interest in the older generation," Auntie Yee exclaimed.

Not long after, a waiter brought towers of neatly stacked bamboo containers and placed them on the glass disc. Nai Nai lifted off one of the lids, and the steam flittered away. The succulent dumplings glistened on their circular white paper.

"Chi-a, chi-a," said Nai Nai, dropping a ha gao dumpling into my bowl. I stabbed it with my chopsticks and stuffed it into my mouth. It was so good. She carried on filling my bowl with different morsels of food and then began to feed herself. Ma just picked at the food and hardly put anything in her bowl.

"Danny is going to spend all of spring break with his grandmother, taking her out and finding fun activities for her to do. Isn't that right, Danny?"

"Sounds mega fun," said Amelia sarcastically.

"Well, at least I don't spend my weekends being taken to loads of boring extracurricular activities," I muttered so the grown-ups couldn't hear. Nai Nai was watching me, though. Then she looked at Amelia, who was pouting.

"Danny, what plans have you got for Nai Nai this week?" Auntie Yee asked.

"Well . . . I thought she might like to try bingo; one of the customers mentioned it," I said.

"Oh no. Definitely not bingo," said Auntie Yee. "It is a crass game played by the lower echelons, Danny. You should take her to lawn bowling; many ladies from the Women's Society go there—she can get light exercise and converse with the right kind of people."

"That sounds good, Clarissa. Thanks for the suggestion," Ma said.

Auntie Yee turned to me. "It will be good for you both. This Easter is the perfect time to bond with her. We look after our elders. It is the Chinese Way." Not her as well . . . I'd had enough of that from Ba.

I dropped my eyes to my bowl and started shoveling in more. Nai Nai had made sure I was fed well. When we finished eating, Auntie Yee got the waiter's attention by waving her hand.

"Mai dan." *Time to pay the bill.*

"Clarissa, let me get it this time," Ma said as she lifted her handbag from the floor.

"No need, no need. I'll pay." Auntie Yee had already gotten her large wallet out of her bag and laid it on the table. She lifted out three crisp new twenty-pound notes and placed them on the small round plate the waiter had brought over with the bill on it. She didn't even glance at the total amount, just put the money on it and handed it back to the waiter. I noticed Nai Nai looking at Ma, who wasn't saying anything. We got ready to leave and walked to the entrance.

Nai Nai whispered something to Ma. Ma's face flushed. We stopped behind Auntie Yee and Amelia.

"Clarissa, we'll get a taxi home. My mother-in-law wants to see the city center some more," said Ma. We'd never gotten a taxi home before.

"Oh . . . if you insist," said Auntie Yee. She seemed upset that she wasn't the one making the decisions. "I'll let you know when I'm coming around next." And on that note, Auntie Yee and Amelia got into their fancy red car. I could tell Auntie Yee's pout meant she wasn't happy; her gaze remained forward as she drove off.

Ma waved. I limply lifted one of my hands. Nai Nai kept babbling.

"What is she saying?" I asked Ma.

"She was saying Auntie Yee and Amelia are like sour grapes—smooth on the outside but hard to digest. I hope Auntie Yee didn't hear; she'd never invite us out again."

Sour grapes. I liked it!

"Come on, let's get out of here," Ma said, smiling at me. "Let's go to the bakery!"

I wanted to give Nai Nai the biggest high five in the land. She got it. She knew. Someone apart from me could finally see Amelia and Auntie Yee for what they really were—horrible!

Nai Nai looked at me and gave me a wink.

# CHAPTER 12

## NOT Bowled Over

**Nai Nai stood at the dining table, packing her bag with fruits of all sizes: a kiwi, a grapefruit, and a bunch of grapes.** Did she think she was going on an expedition or something?

"But do I have to look after her ALL day?" I asked as I played with a piece of toast. Ba put his hands on my shoulders. Nai Nai was humming a ditty.

"Please, Danny, for me?" Ba said. He was almost back to normal, but he needed to take more breaks during the day to rest. "If she's out, then she's not worrying about me and my back. She really wants to spend quality time with you."

"I have a lot of stuff I need to do . . . a math project for one, and other things." Carter had asked me to meet up at the park at two. There was no way I was going to miss playing Blasters for the first time ever. But how was I going to get there if I was *grannysitting* Nai Nai ALL day EVERY day? The sun was shining too.

"Danny, we want her to enjoy her time here with us. Lawn bowling seems like a good idea," Ba said. "She has her free bus pass now, so she can go anywhere local."

I bit my lip as I thought about it. What if people saw me with her? They would think I didn't have any friends and only hung out with my gran.

The phone rang. I picked it up. "Hello?"

"Hi, Danny, it's Ravi. I was wondering if you still wanted me to help you with your math project. You could meet me at the library around three if you want and we can go on the computers there."

I looked over at Ba and Nai Nai, then turned away from them, shielding the receiver with my hands. My belly fluttered. I gulped as my throat suddenly felt dry. I knew Ravi had betrayed me, and I didn't want to see him. But should I come out and tell him that I knew and was upset with him, or should I make up an excuse? I decided on the latter.

"Hiya, erm . . . no. I can't today, Ravi. I have to be with Nai Nai all day. My parents just told me."

Ba smiled and gave me two thumbs up. I wondered if he could tell I was lying.

"Oh, okay, then. I'm sure I can help you come up with something in time for when we go back to school. Maybe another day, then . . ."

He sounded small. I glanced at Ba, who was scrolling through his phone. Nai Nai was piling oranges onto the altar. I felt awkward.

"Ravi, my dad said I have to get off the phone now . . . I've gotta go."

I hung up before Ravi had finished saying goodbye. I didn't need a friend in my life who spread rumors about me. Even if those rumors were true. Ba was looking at me weird.

"You could have stayed on the phone longer, Danny. I didn't say a word."

"It's all right. I want to get outside while it's still nice. You know, so Nai Nai can have a good day out," I lied, again.

"Wonderful," Ba said.

"Gonggong qiche—hao!" Nai Nai said, patting the jacket pocket where she had slid the bus pass. It sounded like she said *Gong gong teacher* to me.

"She's excited to go on the bus," Ba said.

"Okay, we'd better go, then," I said to Nai Nai, a bit deflated. It would be the first time I wouldn't see Ravi over the holidays, but it was his fault, not mine.

"Look after her, Danny. She's the only mother I have," Ba said, smiling.

Nai Nai and I got on the number sixty-three bus, which was a new experience for both of us. Nai Nai wanted to go upstairs and sit in the front seats, even though we only needed to go three stops. As we sat on the top deck, I prepared her for what we were doing.

"I'm going to take you to lawn bowling today. It's full of old people, like you, throwing balls—well, not throwing them, I

guess they roll them?" I held my hands in a ball shape and then proceeded to swing my arm by the side of my body to show her what I was talking about. To reinforce my explanation, I took out a grapefruit from her bag and swung it, but there wasn't much room on the bus to do it properly. I got out my sketchbook and drew a little diagram of what Nai Nai would have to do with the balls.

"This ball you have to get close to the little one . . . and this is your ball, the big one. You throw this one . . . got it?" She nodded. She understood. Ant Gran was quick.

"Okay," she said. Another new word she had learned.

"You will be fine. This is our stop!"

Nai Nai grinned. I pushed the red button and we made our way downstairs. Nai Nai pressed the red button too, multiple times. *Ding! Ding! Ding!* The bus driver gave us an annoyed look when we got off.

The sun was shining bright, and as we neared the bowling club, I could see that the grass appeared flawless, two shades of green mowed in perfect straight lines. Nai Nai couldn't see over the hedges like I could. She would get to see the stripy lawn soon.

We stopped by the entrance and I turned toward her. I did the swinging movement again, but this time added sound effects—*whoosh*—and jumped up and down, doing a pretend victory dance. Nai Nai looked amused.

A group of old people dressed in white clothes and white shoes (and even white hats) were walking on the grass. Nai Nai was wearing her red silk jacket with a golden dragon on the back. I wondered if I should have checked the dress code before we'd come. Nai Nai stood out like a piece of char siu pork in a sea of white potatoes. One man paced up and down, then bent at an angle, his eyes focusing on the grass. I wondered if he was inspecting the grass or whether it was part of some weird bowling ritual. A few of the ladies were chatting on the wooden deck.

As we rounded the corner, I opened the green metal gate that led to the path up to the clubhouse. Nai Nai stopped. She looked at all of the people. They stopped and gawked at us too.

"Hello there," said a lady walking over the grass. "Can we help you? Are you lost?"

"Hi, no, we're not lost. I'm Danny and this is my grandmother. We wanted to sign her up for bowling," I said.

A man stepped onto the grass and threw a white ball. It looked shiny and a lot smaller than the ones with the red stripes on them that the lady was carrying.

"Oh right, I see," the lady said.

"Come on, Marjorie!" shouted another lady. "I'm waiting." They were sure serious about this game.

"I'm sorry. If you go to see George in the clubhouse, he can tell you about the sign-up days for new players. Today we have a mini-tournament, I'm afraid. I really must go, but yes, see George."

"That's great. It's just she's bored at home and it looks good for old"—the lady ignored me and strolled away before I had finished my sentence—"people."

"You don't have to be old to bowl, young man. In fact, you can start at any age, even your age," said a man who had somehow crept up behind me. He was red-faced and had white hair that stuck up like sheep's wool. "I'm George. Come up to the clubhouse and I can give you the forms to fill in and the dates for the next newbies meet, which I'm afraid will not be for two more weeks."

I was disappointed that Nai Nai would have to wait, as we'd already made the journey to get here and I'd be back at school then. George led the way up the path to the white rectangular building beside the green.

I looked around at Nai Nai. She was transfixed by the game that had started on the lawn. *At least she's interested,* I thought. She smiled.

"Nai Nai, come on, this way." I made a hand movement that signified she should follow, but instead of coming with me and George, she started heading to the grass. Then she began speeding up; her trotting became a full-blown run. She put her hand into her bag and pulled out a bright yellow grapefruit. At first I thought she was going to offer it to the ladies as a gesture of friendship—you know, like when you take oranges to a friend's house instead of chocolate because your mom says that Chinese people take fruit as a gift. It was like that, only . . . I could see her eyes. They were focused on the white jack, the small ball that the black ones had to get close to. I screwed up my face, not wanting to see but also not able to take my eyes away.

"Nai Nai!!!!" I began . . . but it was too late. I saw as the sun-like bomb spun into the air and lobbed toward the green. The rest of the bowling ladies just stood there, mouths agape. The man whose game she was joining was running to try to intercept Nai Nai's makeshift ball. I held my breath, my arms outstretched.

"Please, no, not on the green!" George shouted behind me. He started to run too. I ran. Everybody was running!

"Who on earth is that woman?" someone asked.

We were all heading toward my little four-foot grandmother and her grapefruit of destruction. "Ant Gran and Her Mighty Orb" would be the title of this particular comic scene.

I heard a gasp and then I saw it. Her grapefruit . . . spun and spun . . . Its descent was imminent. It hit the grass and slowly bent around to the left. It kissed the white ball and was for all intents and purposes THE WINNER. I smiled even though we had to get out of there, quick.

"She's won . . . with a . . . grapefruit?" one of the ladies noticed, trotting over to the grapefruit and staring at the yellow ball in bewilderment. The woman showed it to the group of bowlers, who were scratching their heads.

"Well, I never, a grapefruit. I wouldn't have spent that money on a new set of balls if I'd known you could win using citrus!" laughed a man with a white comb-over. I'm glad someone was finding it amusing. More onlookers came out of the clubhouse; the people near the lawn were pointing and some of them were glaring at us, a few tutting. We were disturbing the peace, it seemed. It was definitely a sign to exit as quickly as possible.

Rushing back to Nai Nai, I gently ushered her off the lawn, down the path, and out of the gate. She turned and did a victory dance like the one I had shown her earlier. She thought she had won. Someone kicked over her grapefruit. It rolled sadly toward us. I picked it up; it was a little battered and bruised but still eatable, so I popped it into Nai Nai's bag. She was looking around, wondering why we were leaving. I kept nodding and smiling through gritted teeth until we were safely back on the sixty-three bus, heading home. Lawn bowling had failed before it had even begun.

On the way back home, I couldn't look at Nai Nai. How was I supposed to explain that debacle to Ba and Ma? I was the one who had shown her how to throw a fresh grapefruit.

Luckily, Ma and Ba were out when we got home. I didn't want to have to explain why we were back so early; it wasn't even midday. Nai Nai went into the kitchen to make herself a pot of tea and came out with a plate full of guo-tie, or as some people call them, potstickers. I loved them, but Ba never had time to make them for me anymore. He was always too busy.

I grabbed some chopsticks and started dipping the morsels in soy sauce with a bit of cut ginger in it and munching them down. Nai Nai's potstickers were SO good, just like Ba had told me they would be.

I was not doing a very good job of keeping Nai Nai entertained. What activities could she do so that I didn't have to spend my whole spring break with her? Clouds of doubt were still whirling in my mind about whether I would be able to get to see Carter this afternoon.

Perhaps it was a miracle, who knew, but the answer to my prayers passed the window. It was Mrs. Cruikshanks. She had tied her trench coat around her waist and was walking with large earphones on, bopping to music. I ran to the door and opened it.

"Hey, Mrs. Cruikshanks!" I shouted, waving my hands wildly.

"Oh! Hello, young man. I'm listening to the Carpenters—before your time," Mrs. Cruikshanks said, turning around and walking back toward me.

"Did you say before that you go to bingo nearly every afternoon?" I swung the door to and fro, excited that I might have a solution.

Mrs. Cruikshanks leaned in like she had a secret. "Yes, that's right, young Danny. I'm going later."

"GREAT! What time does it start?" If my calculations were right, then I could drop Nai Nai off, run to the park to meet Carter, and be back to pick her up in time for dinner. No one at home would have to know a thing.

"I'm on my way to the nurse; I've got bunions." I didn't know what bunions were and I didn't want to ask. "Bingo starts at two and I will be there. It would take a truck to stop me from going. Why do you ask?"

"Do you think Nai Nai would be able to play?"

"Of course. She's a quick wit, that one. Take her along and I'll see you there later. I've got to rush." With that, Mrs. Cruikshanks started plodding on back down the road, her head bobbing.

A plan was forming in my mind. Bingo with Mrs. Cruikshanks was the perfect and most obvious place for Nai Nai. She could stay there for a couple of hours AND it was close to the park. It was the perfect old people day care. Blaster time for me!

# CHAPTER 13

## Lychees and Bingo Balls

**Nai Nai and I arrived at the Longdale Community Center and followed the arrow signs for bingo, which were in big bold colors.** They led to a large hall where tables were out in rows and the lights were dim. Onstage was a screen; it showed bingo balls bobbing up and down in a glass cube. Pink, green, blue, yellow, and white balls jostling for space and attention.

I had enough money for twelve bingo cards and I got Nai Nai a triple pack of red marker pens, because even I knew that red was lucky in Chinese, and a token for a free cup of tea or coffee and a cookie at break time. These old people had it good. It was warm, they had snacks, and they could basically sit in here all afternoon if they wanted to and play games. Sounded like a good life, if you asked me.

As I returned to the table where I'd left Nai Nai, I saw that a group of old people had gathered. There seemed to be a commotion. I could hear people saying things like "ashamed" and "no way, José." I hurried over with the cards and pens under my arms.

"Hello? Hi? Excuse me? What's going on? Where's my gran?" I squeezed through a wall of white hair and knitted bags.

"Oh, you're with her, are you?" a voice said. It belonged to a very wrinkly lady who had bright blue cotton-candy hair. She was tall and gawked at me like I was a cockroach.

"Yes, I am . . . Nai Nai, are you okay?" I said, getting closer to her. I realized that even though Nai Nai was little, she stood out like a sore thumb because she looked different. I knew how she felt.

"She has to move," another voice chimed in. This time it was a man. He was wearing the same sweater as the blue-haired lady. "We always have these seats, without fail," he asserted. His leg began to twitch. I peered through the crowd of bodies that had formed around us. There were rows upon rows of empty seats.

"But there are loads of other spaces in here," I said. "Can't you sit somewhere else?"

"Cheeky little so-and-so!" said the blue-lagoon lady. I wanted to finger joust all of them away from Nai Nai. She didn't seem so mighty with all of these people jabbering around her.

In fact, she seemed small and a little lost. She was looking around at the angry faces, wondering why they were there. She put her apple core on the table and rummaged in her bag once more. She pulled out a kiwi, offering it to a woman next to her.

"Look, she's new here, okay?" I said. When the woman shook her head, Nai Nai proceeded to get out a small teaspoon, cut the kiwi in half, and begin eating the insides.

I heard a gasp and then a tut.

"You should call management, Enid!" the man in the sweater demanded.

Mrs. Blue Hair ran off with her hand in the air, trying to catch the attention of a lady who was standing by the exit. "Linda! Linda darling . . . over here!"

"Typical foreigners . . . coming here, taking our bingo seats . . ." said a woman who was all gums.

"Excuse me," I said. "I don't mean to be rude and we didn't come to upset anyone. But are these seats reserved, then?"

"Yes, that's where we always sit. Everyone knows that," the man in the sweater said. He was beginning to go red.

Linda was coming over with Mrs. Blue Hair, who was now pointing and moving her hands around. *These bingo people are fanatics,* I thought.

"Hiya. I'm Linda, the manager. Enid tells me that your gran is sitting in her spot. Formally, there aren't any seats that are reserved, but the players generally find spots and like to keep them. It's more of a courtesy, really." The manager was obviously trying to be diplomatic and not cause her regulars to be upset, but also not cause offense to us.

"But all the chairs are the same," I said, feeling angry. Nai Nai should be able to sit wherever she wanted. Even though she'd been driving me up the wall for days, I felt weirdly protective all of a sudden. I put down the bingo cards on the table and placed the markers carefully along the top so they didn't roll off. "I'll speak to her, but she doesn't understand everything I say. But I'll try."

"They don't even speak the same language," I heard someone mutter.

"Nai Nai . . . lai le? I think we could move over there by the window. It's much better, hao?" Using my fingers, I indicated my eyes and the screen.

She nodded. "Hao, hao." Then stood up. Everyone moved back and waited for her to collect her bag of fruit. I picked up the pens and cards and we began to walk away from the rabble. I was relieved to see she was okay and not upset about them ganging up on her. She was a tough old lady, my nai nai. As we moved away to look for a suitable place for her to sit, I saw a person waving frantically from the other side of the room, next to the radiator.

"Coooo–eeee! Over 'ere, love!" a voice piped up. The thick Scottish accent made it clear that Mrs. Cruikshanks was here.

Our savior had arrived. I'd never been so happy to hear the word "Coooo-eeee" in all of my life. Nai Nai recognized Mrs. Cruikshanks and waddled over to her, beaming. I followed.

"Here, you sit by me. You don't want to be over there with that miserable bunch. They act like the hall is theirs and theirs alone. They're territorial at bingo, but you should see them when it's line dancing. They never let anyone join the end of their lines! I'd rather dance by myself, thank you very much!"

Mrs. Cruikshanks began unloading a turquoise quilted bag with red tassels hanging from it. She took out a tall metal flask and a blue plastic plate like the ones you see toddlers eating from. Next to these she placed a plastic cup and a saucer. She didn't stop there. She poked around in what seemed like a bottomless bag and pulled out a packet of five bingo markers and a cushion with cats on it, which she plumped up before plopping it on her chair. Then she got out a packet of chocolate macaroons and a photo of Jesus in a frame, which she arranged at her side. She finally sat down.

"Do you always bring so much . . . you know . . . stuff?" I asked.

"When you get to my age, Danny, you need to be comfortable wherever you go. Trust me, you'll be doing the same when you're seventy-nine." I doubted very much that I would be carrying around a bag with tassels on it and my own cushion.

Nai Nai, not to be outdone, maneuvered past me to the other side of the table, where Mrs. Cruikshanks had made herself at home, and began unloading her handbag. Two kilos of lychees, one orange, another kiwi, and a small flask containing just hot water—that is a Chinese thing. Even my parents never drink ice-cold water. They say it's bad for you. They'd be upset if they knew I loved filling up my water bottle at school from the water fountain in the lobby. Nai Nai sat down next to Mrs. Cruikshanks and patted her friend on the arm.

I put the bingo cards and pens on the table. I looked around the room to see if anyone else had brought as much stuff with them as Mrs. Cruikshanks, and to my surprise most people had bags full of creature comforts. One man in a flat cap was already sucking on a bagful of candy that he had to his right. Another lady with two walking sticks had a sandwich and a bag of chips to munch on.

Putting my hands in my pockets, I turned back to Nai Nai. She was copying everything Mrs. Cruikshanks was doing. Mrs. Cruikshanks straightened up her bingo cards and set her markers by the side. Nai Nai did the same. Mrs. Cruikshanks put her two thumbs up toward Nai Nai and Nai Nai did the same.

I looked up at the big clock on the wall. It was nearly two. Carter had said he would be at the park, waiting for me. I had to go—now!

"Er, Mrs. Cruikshanks, I have to leave now, but I'll be back to collect Nai Nai when it's finished. When should I come back?"

"An hour or so. She'll be as fine as china in a bull shop!" She laughed. I didn't get it. "You go. Tommy's ready now. It's eyes-down time."

"Please don't tell my parents about this. Nai Nai's not supposed to be here and I'm not supposed to let her out of my sight."

"No problem. What they don't know won't hurt 'em."

## CHAPTER 14

# BLASTOFF!

**The park was busy.** With school closed, loads of parents had brought their little kids. Carter was nowhere to be seen. I turned the corner by the bushes. Then, *pffff*, I felt something hit my back. Mitchell was there with two orange plastic Blaster guns. He was wearing an ammo belt full of foam pellets.

"You're late," he said, smirking. "That means you get a forfeit and I can hit you with as many pellets as I want for one minute."

"Ahhh, that's not fair, is it? Where's Carter?" I was sure Carter had told me the others would be nicer. Shooting me in the back didn't seem like a good way to start.

"Life isn't fair. That's what my parents keep telling me." Mitchell proceeded to hit me in the belly with five pellets.

Then he handed me a Blaster half the size of his and a handful of pellets.

I shoved the pellets into my hoodie pocket. "Is this the only one you have for me? It's a bit . . . small. Don't you have a larger one?"

"Nope . . . Mitchell called dibs on the other one," said Carter as he jogged over. "My mom said we could all go back to my place after. Can you come?"

"No, I have to go get my . . . I mean, I've got to pick up something afterward."

I aimed at the center of the slide to practice my aim. Jay Jay ran over; he was wearing a khaki T-shirt like Mitchell. Both minions were here. Ergh.

"Are you ready for some aiming gaming? You're on my team, Danny," Carter said, grinning. "You didn't hit Danny already, did you?"

"No, no, we just had some friendly banter, that's all." Mitchell swiveled on his heel and ran off. His neon-yellow sneakers were like beacons in the grass. "But now it's on."

For the first time in ages I felt free and was having fun running around and hiding. Carter was a pretty good shot. But that was probably because all he did was play computer games and shoot his Blaster gun on the weekends. It was good not worrying about Nai Nai following me, being alone, or being stuck in the apartment thinking about how bad I was at math. I hit Jay

Jay in the butt and that was five points. Carter was impressed that I was as good as he was. To be honest, I'd never played before and wasn't sure I'd be any good, but our team was winning. We decided to give the others a head start for round two. Mitchell and Jay Jay had an extra ten seconds to run and hide.

"Ready or not, we're coming!" shouted Carter.

That was when I saw him.

Sir Ravi of Longdale.

Oh no! I'd told him I was with Nai Nai all day. He was with his mom and little brother. Vishal was running over to the swings not far from where we were playing Blasters. Ravi and his mom were talking. I ducked into a hedge and crouched down. I could hear my breathing; it was shallow and fast.

My feet were beginning to hurt because I was squatting on tiptoe. Carter gave me a wave. He pointed toward the playground, where Mitchell and Jay Jay were hiding on top of the climbing frame. I knew that if I came out of the bushes, Ravi would see me. Carter wasn't going to invite me again if I didn't move. But Ravi was the one who should be apologizing to me. This was a mess. Frozen to the spot, I shook my head.

"What's the matter? They're sitting ducks," Carter insisted.

I tried to think of an excuse. "You go first. I'll wait and get anyone who runs off."

Carter looked out. He clocked Ravi and his family, who were now near the playground.

"Aren't you going to say hello to your best friend?" Carter said.

"Who do you mean?" I kept my head and gaze down, hoping that Carter would leave me alone.

"Danny's over here!" Carter yelled. He was standing up tall and pointing his Blaster gun down at me. Mitchell and Jay Jay also saw our now-exposed hiding place. They began to run over to where we were.

"Shhhhh," I whispered. I hunched my shoulders. I looked up and saw Ravi squinting in my direction. He pushed up his glasses. He'd spotted me. I stood up. For a second he looked surprised; then, when he saw me holding one of Carter's Blasters, his face changed. He pulled up his hood and turned his back, shoving his hands into his pockets.

His mom said something to him, but he shook his head. I could tell he wanted to leave.

"Ahhh, he's not happy with someone," Carter said, then laughed.

"Ravi was the one who started it," I said. "Come on, let's keep playing." I glanced over at Ravi. He looked like he didn't know what to do with himself. He peered at me, then at Carter and Mitchell.

"I'm gonna get you!" Jay Jay shouted, coming toward me. I had to run for it or I'd get hit. I could see Mitchell. I ran and dived into the sandbox and pulled the trigger as I was diving.

The pellet hit Mitchell in the back. He turned with a scowl on his face. My jacket was being pulled at. I looked down and Vishal was tugging on the corner of it.

"Hey, Vishal."

"What are you doing? Can I play?"

"No, sorry. It's not my Blaster."

"Can I play if Ravi plays?"

I felt a stab in my chest. Ravi wouldn't want to play with me anymore . . . probably.

Ravi was coming toward us.

"Vishal, get out of there. Come on now!" His voice sounded strained. He wouldn't look at me.

"But Danny is here. Can we play too?" Vishal was trying to take the Blaster out of my hands.

"No! Let's go. We don't want to play with someone who lies. Come on!"

Mitchell was now running into the bushes. Carter was chasing Jay Jay around by the memorial benches with dead flowers tied to them.

"I'm not . . . Ravi . . . it's just that I wanted to . . ." How could I explain to someone I'd lied to that it was fun to play with Carter? It was different from playing with Ravi.

"You're busy with your grandmother, huh?"

"I was busy with her . . . earlier."

Vishal ran off in the direction of the swings.

"But now you're here . . . with them." He lifted his chin toward the boys as they ducked and weaved through the bushes.

Ravi bit his lip and pushed up his glasses. He did that when he was nervous.

"Ravi! Can you push Vishal on the swing? I have a call!" Ravi's mom lifted her phone to her ear.

"Bye, traitor," Ravi said, turning and walking away from me.

"Me, the traitor? You're the one who made me look like a fool at school. You're the traitor! You told everyone about Nai Nai sharing my bunk bed."

Ravi looked at me. "It just slipped out. I didn't mean to tell Tia. But you blatantly lied and said you were hanging out with your gran all day."

My tongue felt tied, and my mind went blank. I didn't know what to say. It was true, I had lied. Before I could say another word, Ravi turned and left. He walked over to the swings, lifted Vishal into the seat, and gave a half-hearted push.

"Higher!"

Ravi pushed and Vishal swung into the sky. His mom put her phone into her bag and took over pushing her younger son.

Carter ran by and patted me on the back. "Danny! Come on, they're running to the bandstand!" he said.

Picking up my Blaster with two hands, I jogged away from the playground and my former best friend. "What time is it?" I asked.

"Dunno," said Carter, shouting over the park's noise. "Jay Jay, what's the time on your phone?"

"Nearly three thirty!"

"Man, I've gotta go pick up my . . . go to the shop."

"All right. Come out tomorrow if you want."

"Thanks, I'll try to make it," I said, handing him the Blaster he'd lent me.

"Did you start your math presentation yet?" Carter asked, taking the Blaster.

"Not yet. Haven't had time. What about you?"

"Yeah, I'm gonna do it on Fortnite . . . but it's not finished yet." Fortnite? I should have known. If Carter wasn't on his Blaster guns, he was playing Fortnite at home.

"Sounds . . . interesting," I said. Even Carter had an idea. I was pretty much the only one in the whole class who had no clue what he was doing.

"I'll tell you about it tomorrow. See ya," Carter said. He, Mitchell, and Jay Jay laughed their way toward the street on the other side of the park, where they lived.

It was what I'd wanted, to play with Carter, so why did I feel so sick inside?

# CHAPTER 15

# HAO-SI! (A.K.A. HOUSE!)

**I was out of breath from running so fast back to the bingo hall to pick up Nai Nai.** My chest hurt from the sharp intake of breath when I finally arrived. The doors were wide open and Nai Nai stood up from the bench in the lobby.

"Dan Dan-a!" she exclaimed. In her arms she had a bottle of perfume, a cuddly toy, a bag full of ladies' tights, and a white envelope.

"Where have you been?" Mrs. Cruikshanks asked. "You've missed the show!"

"What?"

"Your nanny . . . she's something else! In all my years coming, I've never seen fingers so fast. Nothing like it, I tell you. She was banging spots on all of the cards like she was swatting midges at Loch Lomond. Bam bam bam."

"What, she actually won all that stuff?"

"Won? She got bingo four times and house once—when it mattered, mind you. She got some little things and an amazing two hundred pounds' worth of vouchers for Freezer City. Imagine how much shrimp cocktail you can get for two hundred quid!"

"Hao-si!" shouted Nai Nai.

"Howse?" I repeated.

"House . . . it's when you get all of the numbers on the board. She got every single one of them little numbers. Enid and her cranky friends were none too pleased, I can tell you now. Enid was practically sulking. Her hair wasn't the only thing that was blue!"

"She should dye it green . . . with envy," I chimed in. I was so proud of Nai Nai. Her first time at bingo and she'd cleaned up. I was always worrying that I would mess up. That was one of the reasons I didn't like math, because I was scared I would get the wrong answer. Sometimes I didn't try things in the first place. But Nai Nai just tried things even though she didn't know what they were. She went for it at lawn bowling and she took a chance at bingo. Now look at her: She was so happy.

Nai Nai's eyes sparkled. She pushed the cuddly toy into Mrs. Cruikshanks's hands—the furry gift was well received.

Then she sprayed herself all over from head to toe with the perfume she'd won—it was called Poison. What a silly name for a perfume! Mrs. Cruikshanks coughed and stepped back, putting her hand to her mouth. I began coughing too.

"Jesus, Mary, Mother of God! Not so much!"

"When are you going to bingo again, Mrs. Cruikshanks?" I asked.

"When am I NOT going to be there, more like. I go every afternoon if I can. Some mornings I like to help at the charity shop—Dogs for the Blind. The dogs aren't blind—it's the people who are blind—but they're not in the shop. Then Thursday mornings I'm at a tea dance. But the afternoons are for bingo. I can't get enough of it."

"You do a lot of stuff."

"When you get to my age, you've got to keep busy. Mind you, next Tuesday, I've got a woman coming to cut my toenails. Anyway . . . she's a star, your nan. Your folks must be proud—she's got all of her faculties up top." Mrs. Cruikshanks tapped her own head.

"Yes, both of them are very proud." I imagined what they would really say if they found out that I had left Nai Nai here with Mrs. Cruikshanks and, secondly, that she was playing bingo.

"They're both extremely happy that Nai Nai has a friend like you. So cultured and loyal." *You're going over the top, Danny!*

135

Hearing Ma saying stuff like that to Auntie Yee must have been rubbing off on me.

"Oh, I have to tell you. You know what she did? I think it's her lucky charm. She was eating those round slimy things. Leeches."

"Lychees."

"Yes, that's what I said. She was pelting out the black bullets from her mouth and shooting them into a pile on the table. She offered me one, but to be honest, they give me the heebie-jeebies."

Nai Nai was sniffing her Freezer City vouchers.

"No, no, Nai Nai . . ." I said, taking them from her hands. "You can't spend those if you ruin them."

"You better take her to Freezer City and show her what to do with them . . . GO GET YOURSELF A SEAFOOD PLATTER, LOVE!" Mrs. Cruikshanks gave Nai Nai a gentle hug around the shoulders. And then Nai Nai turned and grabbed Mrs. Cruikshanks and hugged her close.

Taking Nai Nai to Freezer City was a revelation. Nai Nai kept opening all of the deep freezers and sticking her head into them to see what was lurking inside. Her belly nudged against the white panels as her feet lifted off the floor. I imagined her falling forward and being trapped in a deep freezer forever. Ant Gran cryogenically frozen for eternity! That would solve my issues and she would be permanently out of my room. But I was starting to feel a bit different about her. She wasn't so bad after all. And now that she was starting to make friends and get out of the apartment, things would change. Maybe I wouldn't have to be the one to always chaperone her places. Maybe Mrs. Cruikshanks would be kind enough to take her around. Nai Nai might like to do some of the other activities that Mrs. Cruikshanks did too, like the tea dance. Dancing and tea sounded like something she would enjoy.

We arrived back home after six with five shopping bags full of frozen stuff, like chocolate chip ice cream (that was what I had picked), and Nai Nai had found a whole salmon that still had its eyes. She pointed to its eyes and said, "Hao chi." *Delicious.* Eyes. Fish eyes. Delicious? Gross. How were we even related?

Ma was wiping the counter when we got home. Nai Nai rushed forward to show her the bounty from the bingo hall.

"Wow, how did she get all of this stuff?" Ma took one of the bags and opened it. "Fish and perfume?"

"Oh, she won it."

Nai Nai took the food into the kitchen, where we had two large freezers.

"At bowling? They have prizes at the bowling club?"

"Er . . . yes . . ." Why hadn't I just told Ma the truth? "They were having a raffle and she won. They pulled her ticket out of the raffle tin."

"All of that stuff from one raffle ticket?"

"Uh-huh."

"So you two had a nice day? You were there a long time. I bet she was good at bowling, wasn't she?"

"Yeah, brilliant, actually." That wasn't a lie.

"And the people? They were nice?"

"Mostly . . ." I didn't want to tell Ma about being run off the bowling green, or the gang of oldies at bingo who'd made Nai Nai move seats. Ba came through the front carrying a box of bean sprouts. He put them on the counter, which annoyed Ma. Then he gave me a squeeze and ruffled my hair. "Hey! How was your day?"

"He's been with Nai Nai all day; they only just got in. They're getting along nicely," Ma said.

"I told you. Having her here is really good for you. She can teach you lots of things about our history and culture. She won't be around forever. You're making your ba really happy. Well done, Danny. I'm really proud of you," Ba said, disappearing with his box into the kitchen.

"You're welcome." Surely the little white lies were fine. Nai Nai had enjoyed her first bingo experience with Mrs. Cruikshanks while I was out playing with my cool new friends. But I missed Ravi. I wished we weren't mad at each other. I felt bad that I'd lied to him now—even if he had told everyone about Nai Nai and me sharing bunk beds.

# CHAPTER 16

# SKATE PARK CONFESSIONS

**Spring break seemed to be zooming by.** The next morning, I stared at my math book, willing it to send me telepathic thoughts about what to do for my presentation. Ravi was doing a fractions hip-hop thing. Carter was doing something about probability and Fortnite. Tia wouldn't tell me what she was doing. And Amelia definitely wasn't going to show me her project. Time was slipping through my fingers like sand and still my mind was a blank.

Ba's back was much better, but Ma still needed to help him with the food preparation and the trips to the wholesaler to buy supplies. After lunch, Ma handed me and Nai Nai a big chocolate egg each. They were wrapped in deep purple foil with puzzles on the back of their cardboard boxes. She said we could eat them right away, since we didn't really celebrate Easter. I sat at the dining table, unwrapping mine. Nai Nai pushed hers toward me and said something to Ma.

"She said 'too sweet.' You can have hers, too. She's happy with her fruit."

I looked at Nai Nai. "Thanks!" She tottered off upstairs.

"Are you taking her to bowling again today?"

"Yes, we're heading over there now."

Earlier, Nai Nai had nudged me when I was in my room cleaning up. She'd said, "Hao-si?" which meant she wanted to go to bingo again. I'd nodded but put my finger to my lips, hoping she wouldn't tell my parents where we were going.

"You're being so kind, Danny, spending your free time with Nai Nai. It's what we always wanted."

I squirmed in my seat. Of course, I was going to take her to bingo and then leave her to meet up with Carter again.

"I've got one for Ravi, too," said Ma, holding up another chocolate egg. "When will you be seeing him?" I looked around the table and saw she had actually bought a large box full of the eggs.

"Oh, I don't know. He's been really busy with family stuff, I think. I'll be sure to give it to him when I do see him, though," I said, not knowing when I was going to see my ex–best friend again.

I stood up as Nai Nai appeared with her coat on and the woolly hat that I didn't wear.

She filled her bag with her favorite fruits and we left for bingo.

Mrs. Cruikshanks greeted us and took Nai Nai in. As I left the community center, I noticed a red Mercedes slowly driving by. It reminded me of something, but I couldn't put my finger on it. I turned and headed to the park. I hoped Ravi wasn't going to be there again. Yesterday was pure squirminess. I had to put him in the back of my mind and try to have some fun. At least I didn't have to lie now or pretend I didn't want to hang out with Carter.

As I neared the concrete ramps, I noticed Carter had brought his black stunt scooter, and a slightly shorter blue one was leaning against the metal fence. His dad was driving off.

"Hey, Carter," I said, lifting my hand. I noticed he wasn't wearing a helmet or kneepads.

"My brother said you could use his scooter. I wasn't sure if you had one. It's over there."

"Thanks. I do have one, but it's from when I was little." Ravi and I weren't really into these kinds of physical activities. I'd once tried Ravi's sister's skateboard, and my butt was not happy about it when I fell off. But if I wanted to keep playing with Carter, I would have to try to enjoy this stuff a bit more. Scootering was much easier than skateboarding, so I thought I would be all right.

Carter showed me some of his moves. He was really good at spinning the scooter in midair. I hesitated when it was my turn on the skate ramp. I stared down from the top. It looked like a long way to fall.

"Er . . . you can go again, Carter," I said, my toes hanging off the edge. "I'll just scooter over there." I pointed to the flat area next to us.

"Come on, Danny. Don't think, just go." Carter gave me a little nudge and I whooshed down the concrete and whizzed back up the other side. My heart was racing. I'd done it without falling! And it was cool! I turned and grinned at Carter, who gave me a thumbs-up.

We carried on scootering for a while and then sat and rested on the picnic benches. I'd brought my backpack with some cookies. I gave one to Carter, who scarfed it down in a couple of bites. Then I got out my sketchbook. I looked over at Carter to see if he was going to ask me about it, but he was too busy eating the crumbs that had fallen into his lap. I shoved my cookie into my mouth and grabbed my pens. I had to draw a snail on a skateboard going down a ramp before I forgot about it. I started to sketch.

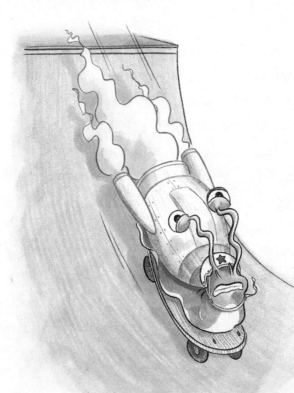

"Do you wanna do some speech bubbles for this new comic I'm drawing." I asked Carter. "It's called Stunt Snail?" I thought he'd be into this one, because he was good at scootering and doing stunts.

"Nah," Carter said, peering over. "Not my thing."

"Oh okay, right." I gazed at my sketchbook. It was a really good character, but there was no one here to appreciate it apart from me. I shaded in the helmet that I had given Stunt Snail. It had a star on it.

"Why's it got that fire coming out of its butt?" Carter asked.

"It's half rocket, half snail, and he's on a skateboard, and there's fire, that's him burning rocket fuel."

"Don't you think it's a bit . . . you know . . ."

"A bit what?" Awesome? Cool? Legendary?

"It's a bit . . . well . . . babyish? We're going to middle school soon."

"But I like drawing," I told him, deflated.

"Put it away. The boys are here," Carter said. Mitchell and Jay Jay were sauntering over the grass toward us.

I shut my sketchbook and shoved it into my backpack.

"Have you asked him?" Mitchell said, raising his eyebrows and tilting his head toward me.

"Not yet . . ." Carter said.

"What is it?" I asked, feeling like I should leave the park and just head to the community center to get Nai Nai.

"Well, being as us three have been kind enough to play with you . . ." Carter began.

"Yeah, we thought you could help us with our math presentations," Jay Jay said, wiping his nose with the back of his hand.

"My mom said all Chinese people are good at math and that we should hang out with the Chinese boys in our school, and you are the only one in our year," Mitchell said. "I think you owe us, Chung."

Stereotype city or what? I wanted to burst out laughing. Then the next second I wanted to cry.

"Well . . . sorry to burst your bubbles, guys, but I'm no good at math." I could sense things were turning sour. Very sour.

"Are you saying my mom is wrong?" Carter asked. "But I've let you use my stuff."

"Carter, honestly, I'm not good at math. I can't help you." My fingers began to shake as I put my backpack straps on. It was definitely time to go.

"Can't or won't?" Carter asked.

"Really nice seeing you all . . . Gotta go."

"Okay, well, beware, Chung. Once you make an enemy of us, it's for life," Carter said.

He pointed his two fingers at me and then toward his own eyes, then back at me. I skulked away and headed for the community center.

# CHAPTER 17

## BUSTED

**Ma was folding sheets on the dining table behind the counter when Nai Nai and I got home from bingo.** Nai Nai took off her shoes and went upstairs.

Ma looked at me sternly. "I know where you've been, Danny."

*Uh-oh*, I thought.

"I specifically told you to take her to lawn bowling. It's a gentle sport and she can get exercise. I did not tell you to take her to bingo." I could hear echoes of Auntie Yee.

"But . . ."

"Ah. Let me finish. Clarissa called me. She saw you leaving Nai Nai outside the bingo place. She was all alone." I knew I recognized that red car.

"It's a community center and she wasn't alone. There's . . . a . . . community. Nothing bad happened to her."

"Clarissa said you weren't watching her; she saw you in the park with a pack of boys." A *pack of boys*? She'd been spying on me.

"Do you always need to listen to what Auntie Yee says?"

"You were supposed to look after Nai Nai, not leave her with strangers."

"Mrs. Cruikshanks isn't a stranger," I pleaded.

"There is nothing more to say. You will go to your room. You are grounded until you go back to school."

I wanted to scream, *I DON'T HAVE A ROOM ANYMORE!* But I didn't.

I stomped upstairs to my—correction, *our*—room. I tried to slam the door, but Nai Nai's dressing gown was hung over the edge of it, so it made no noise. I couldn't even bang the door right! I flopped onto my duvet and stuffed my face into my pillow.

Things couldn't get any worse. Could they? Normally, Ravi'd be the one I'd call and we'd draw a comic about it and have a laugh. But things with us were a mess right now.

Nai Nai's face appeared from over the side of the top bunk.

"Dan Dan okay?" she said.

"No, I'm not okay."

She scrambled down the ladder and came to sit next to me on my bed. She patted my knee.

"It's complicated, Nai Nai. Ma said no more bingo. No more hao-si. Danny, I mean, I am . . . in trouble. How can I explain it to you? How can I explain it ALL to you?"

I kinda wished I had picked up more Chinese, because in times like these, it would be good to tell someone how I felt. Right now I felt like a building was sitting on my shoulders. I'd seen Nai Nai with Mrs. Cruikshanks. She had no idea what her friend was saying, but she was listening all the same. That was like Ravi: he was a good listener. Not like Carter.

I picked up my sketchbook from my backpack and started flicking through it. I came across the Ant Gran, Supervillain, comic and quickly kept turning the pages, hoping Nai Nai didn't see that one. I flipped to the back page—the blank page stared up at me. Nai Nai picked up my pencil case and rummaged through it. She pulled out a pencil and took my book. I almost grabbed it back in case she saw the drawings I had done of her. But I let her take it. She drew a heart with a smiley face. She was telling me she loved me.

I drew an angry Ma, mouth open, baring her teeth and yelling. Then I drew some bingo balls and crossed them out like a DO NOT ENTER sign. An arrow indicated what the consequences for me were—a bed here, a few bars there, my sad face. She could see from my sketch that I was grounded in my room.

"Then there's the math project . . . shuxue—that's what you call it, isn't it? No good. I'm awful at math, Nai Nai, and I

don't know what to do. Ba and Ma will be disappointed in me if I keep being in the bottom of my class." I drew some addition totals and other math symbols and then scribbled them all out. "I bet you never had any trouble like this in China, did you?"

Lastly, I drew a picture of me and Ravi. Ravi was in one corner and I was in another. It would have been cheesy to draw a broken heart, but that was kinda how I felt. It had only been a few days, but I wanted him back. I wanted him to do my speech bubbles, to play finger jousting, to come up with more excellent mutant-dragon ideas. Being in the cool-kid gang wasn't all that fun anyway. But I guess you don't know until you try something.

"There's not much you can do about Ravi. I have to go say I'm sorry. Make it up to him. It's good to have a friend who understands you, isn't it?"

Nai Nai put her arm around me and gave me a side hug. I laid my head on her shoulder.

"Yes, we're friends, Nai Nai. I'm sorry to you, too. You don't know what I've done." I thought about the pictures I had drawn of Ant Gran being catapulted into the jaws of a dragon. I would get rid of them.

She rubbed my arm and held my face in her hands. When she smiled, the whole of her face, wrinkles and all, lifted and it was like her face was one big smile. She got up and stretched her arms high above her head like she was about to take off, like an Ant Gran Superhero. I felt much better just from showing her that I had a lot on my mind. It wasn't that I was just a bad grandson. I had been quite selfish. Ba and Ma were both right: we didn't know how long she would be here for. I had to make the most of it.

She padded out of the room with her hands on her hips. Following her downstairs, I crept to the bottom step and stayed hidden. What was she doing? In the kitchen, I could hear loud voices. Nai Nai was babbling, but it was bordering on shouting. She'd always been so calm since she'd been here. Ma was saying something and Ba was trying to keep the peace. I heard my name, but other than that, I couldn't really make out what was going on. Just then the kitchen door opened and Ma came out.

"Danny! Come down!"

I ran back upstairs to the halfway point and then started coming down, making heavy footsteps to pretend I wasn't being sneaky.

"Did you call me?" I asked, trying to look like I hadn't been eavesdropping.

"Yes, Nai Nai has spoken to us and she wants you to be ungrounded. She said it was her idea to go to bingo. Is that true?" She'd lied for me?

"Well . . ." I saw Nai Nai slink out of the kitchen. A hopeful smile lit up her face, her eyebrows raised as if to say, *Tell them yes!* She urged me with her nodding head.

"Kinda . . . yeah, I suppose so. It's just at bowling . . . she had this grapefruit . . ."

"Ah . . . no need to explain further. You are ungrounded. BUT . . . you don't take her there again—you understand me? I think Clarissa is right. It's not a good place for her."

"Understood, no more bingo."

I was ungrounded—*thank you, Nai Nai.* When my mom's head was turned, I looked at Nai Nai and gave her a thumbs-up. I couldn't believe she had gone in there and given them a piece of her mind. That was definitely the Chinese Way—elders always won.

## NO MORE YEES!

**I flipped the OPEN sign on the front door and then headed back behind the counter.** Business was slow, probably because it was raining. People liked to stay home when it was wet out. I could hear Auntie Yee's heels clicking before I saw her. What was she doing here?

"Su Lin, I'm here!" she chirped while holding the door open for Amelia, who followed like a soggy rain cloud, her eyes rolling. She and her mother were in fuchsia today.

"She invited herself," Ba whispered as he came through to the counter area with a large plate of expensive raw jumbo shrimp from the side storage area; he went into the kitchen without saying another word. He was probably annoyed that he had to cook extra food for them when they never invited us around for dinner. Auntie Yee sat down and took her coat off. I could hear Ba banging the wok around more than usual.

Amelia was told to hang out with me, so she reluctantly followed me upstairs. We passed the living room, where Nai Nai was watching a show about baking cakes. I was still mad at Amelia and her mom for telling on me and Nai Nai for going to bingo.

"How is it sharing your room with your nai nai?" Amelia asked as she moved my clothes from the chair to the floor. Then she sat down with her tablet in her hand, swiping right and then right again.

"You and your mom are snitches. Nai Nai was enjoying herself at bingo and you had to go and ruin it!"

"It was our duty to inform your mom I saw your nai nai there all alone. Goodness knows what could have happened to her. We were being good citizens."

"I was grounded for two weeks because of you! Luckily, I got out of it."

"Whatever. I just want to get out of here. I don't know why my mom bothers coming here at all."

"She comes because she's bored and has got nothing better to do than poke her nose into other people's lives!"

The door to my room creaked open and Auntie Yee was

standing there, her face as pink as her outfit. "You despicable boy! How dare you be so rude?"

Ma's head appeared around the door. "Food is ready. What is going on here?"

"Your son has been saying things about me—poking my nose in. I came here out of good faith, Su Lin."

"I'm sure we can work this out. Danny doesn't mean it." Ma was getting flustered and her face was going red.

"If this is how you raise the boy, then he will not amount to anything—mark my words."

Ma looked at me, disappointed yet again. I just couldn't seem to do the right thing.

"Danny, apologize right now," Ma said.

"I won't say I'm sorry. 'Amelia's this and Amelia's that.' Auntie Yee only comes here to—" I was cut off by Mrs. High-and-Mighty herself.

"He's a troublemaker, Su Lin," said Auntie Yee. "I told you that school was no good. You should have gone private or at least to a good disciplined Catholic school. Look how your child behaves and look at Amelia. There is no comparison. You get what you pay for." Was she talking about me or the schools? I was confused and angry.

"Amelia's mean and we all know where she gets that from!" I shouted. "You always take her side, Ma!"

"Danny, you stop this right now." Ma was clearly embarrassed.

"Amelia is not a mean girl," announced Auntie Yee. "She is delightful, and you are a disgrace. Su Lin, how can you raise such a foulmouthed boy? Amelia, come downstairs; we're going." With that, Auntie Yee grabbed Amelia's arm. Her lips were pursed. Her eyes gleamed daggers toward me. Then they disappeared downstairs.

"Wait! Wait, Clarissa!" Ma's mouth hung open for a second or two; then she turned to me. I could see her brain was figuring out whether she should try to find a peaceful solution or admonish me. She chose the latter.

"Danny! I can't believe what you said to Clarissa. I am so disappointed in you."

I looked at the floor.

Ba appeared with two trays of garlic jumbo shrimp, shells still on. Their forlorn black eyes bulged, and their long pink antennae bobbed around "Where did Clarissa and Amelia go? I've cooked these snacks for them."

"They left," said Ma, edging her way past Ba and downstairs, clearly upset that I had caused her to lose face.

"Who is going to eat these, then?" he said, staring at me.

"Nai Nai and I will eat them," I said.

Ba passed me the trays, grateful that his cooking was

not going to be wasted. "Your ma will be okay. She doesn't realize that Clarissa can never be pleased. But she won't hear it from me. Or from you. She has to see it herself, in her own time."

"Thanks, Ba," I said.

I walked into the living room. Nai Nai was on the sofa. She turned off the TV when she saw me.

We sat in silence, peeling the prawns and making a big pile of pink shell pieces in the middle of the table. They were juicy and really garlicky, just how I liked them. Even though Nai Nai couldn't speak back to me, I felt like she understood that I wanted to be me. Danny Chung. I desperately needed someone I could talk to. My fingers were greasy, so I couldn't draw this time, but just talking would help me feel less guilty about what had happened. I'd blown up, but it wasn't just because of the Yees; it was everything.

"It's not that I was making stuff up, Nai Nai—you know how they are. Every single visit, Auntie Yee makes me feel small." I held up a shrimp I'd just shelled. "Imagine this is me. I've got no shell, no protection, I'm defenseless, and Auntie Yee is like a big shark who is always out to get me." I bit off half of the shrimp's body. And chomped.

Nai Nai smiled and did the same to her shrimp. "Hao chi . . . hao chi."

Ba popped his head around the living room door.

"You okay?" he asked.

"Yeah, fine. I think I need some fresh air," I replied.

"Well, if you're going out, you can take Nai Nai to Mr. Potempa's. She wanted you to help her carry some watermelons and more lychees home."

"Sure, come on, Nai Nai. Let's go," I said.

# CHAPTER 19

## Eureka!

**The Global Mini-Mart was looking especially tidy today.** Mr. Potempa had arranged the fruits and vegetables outside in a rainbow arc with reds at the top, followed by orange produce like butternut squash and satsumas. Bananas and lemons followed, then green, blue, and purple fruit at the bottom. In the middle green row was the fantastic spiky vegetable that we'd seen on Nai Nai's first visit to the shop. I picked it up and started to feel its pointy edges. Nai Nai took it from me and put it in her basket. She gave me a wink and I smiled. It looked as if a broccoli and a cauliflower had had a baby *and* it was injected with alien juice. The sign reminded me: ROMAN-ESCO CAULIFLOWER. I was so glad she was going to buy it this time. I was sure it would inspire me to draw something zany and creative.

Mr. Potempa appeared in the doorway with his broom.

"Afternoon, Danny and Danny's grandmother. I see you're going to buy one of the special cauliflowers today. I have a discount on apricots."

We went in and walked around the store. Nai Nai chatted away to herself, feeling at ease, and tried a few samples before she bought them. We headed home, our arms heavy with fresh fruits and vegetables.

After unpacking the bags and filling up the fruit bowls, we sat at the dining table. Ba sat down next to us.

"Ma reminded me you have a math project to do. And that Amelia is in the same competition. Whatever happens, just try your best."

"Yeah, but I can't think of a single thing to present. It's got to be fun and entertaining. It's just, math is hard and I like drawing."

"I know you like drawing, Danny, but you need to focus on other things too." Nai Nai was watching us talk. She said something to Ba and he said something back. "Nai Nai said math is a state of mind. And there is always a way through." Ba looked as confused as I felt. "Anyway, I need to go break some eggs!

Dinner in thirty minutes, okay? You'll figure it out. Math is in our blood, remember!"

I was feeling overwhelmed and stressed that I hadn't even begun my math project. *Math was in our blood?* The only thing in my blood was platelets. What I needed to do was draw. Sitting down at the table with my sketchbook and pen made me feel calm. Scanning the room, I looked for inspiration. What should I draw? Nai Nai's funny cauliflower was sitting right in front of me in the fruit bowl, like a pointy beacon.

I began with the outline of the strange vegetable. My pencil zoomed all over, a jagged bit here, a spiky bit there. The word that kept popping into my head as I was sketching was "alien";

it looked like it was extraterrestrial. The Vegetable from Outer Space. I drew some moons orbiting the edges of the paper. A little Martian with a spring-onion antenna flew around on a turbo mushroom.

Nai Nai glanced over my shoulder. Then I heard her go, "Ah!"

"What is it, Nai Nai?" I asked. I turned to see what she was doing.

She started waving her hands like she had won at bingo. I was confused. She grabbed the Romanesco cauliflower from the fruit bowl and laid it in front of me, pointing at it like it was some magic object. She kept jigging around like she literally had ants in her Ant Gran pants.

"Danny-ah!!!" She kept tapping the drawing.

"Cauliflower?" I asked. "What are you trying to say?"

Nai Nai grabbed my math textbook from school and rushed through the pages. She was searching for something. What was she trying to tell me? Then she found it. The page said:

*Fibonacci—Math in Nature.* On the page was a picture of the Romanesco cauliflower and other plants and flowers. It explained how math was all around us, even in nature. Nai Nai tapped my sketchbook and then my math book, then brought her hands together very slowly in front of me and crisscrossed her fingers together. Together? Bring together?

"Integrate them? Math and drawing?"

Nai Nai wrote down the Fibonacci sequence for me so I could copy it. It was a series of numbers: 0, 1, 1, 2, 3, 5, 8, 13, 21, 34 . . . It was quite simple when you thought about it. The next number was found by adding up the two numbers before it. It got bigger and bigger the more you added.

Then Nai Nai drew a grid that showed how it would look when we made squares with those widths, and how you could keep expanding it and expanding it. Then, with a red pen, she traced a spiral.

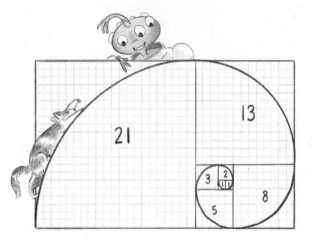

I was loving it; yes, I, Danny Chung, was enjoying something related to math. She picked up the cauliflower again and showed me how each floret was like the spiral pattern, because the florets had to turn and create new turns. It kept going and going and you were left with a beautiful thing.

My math textbook showed a sunflower and the way its seeds had a similar special formation. I sketched that, too. My mind was full to the brim with ideas of what I could draw and what I could say.

Nai Nai patted me on the back. I stood up and gave her the biggest hug EVER!

"Thanks, Nai Nai. We're a good team. Lucky Dragons!"

# CHAPTER 20

## MEMORIES OF A LIFETIME

**Nai Nai and I spent the rest of the evening researching other things in nature that demonstrated the Fibonacci sequence.** For the first time in ages, I felt like I could really do something great. I had a new formula to work with:

> my drawing skills
> +
> Nai Nai's big math brain
> _____
> a cool math presentation.

Perhaps I *could* do math after all.

"Nai Nai, this has been the weirdest few weeks," I said to her. "Ravi and I have fallen out. Carter and his crew were just using me. Ma was trying to make me be like Amelia; I'm a big disappointment to her. And my room, which I thought was going to get an awesome makeover, was somewhere I had no privacy when you moved in. But right now you're the only one who accepts me as I am. Ma and Ba never have time for me and are always working. It's just too much, you know?"

"Danny-a. Hao, hao-a." She looked into my eyes and patted my shoulder; then she ushered me to our bedroom. She stood on the chair and pulled down her suitcase, which was on top of my wardrobe. She laid it on the floor and unzipped it. Inside was a large tatty envelope. The corners were ripped, and it had some Chinese characters on it. Sitting on the floor with her legs wide, she poured out the contents. It was a stack of old photos: mostly black-and-white ones, a few in color. Some had been damaged by age; the sides were brown and gnarly. There were also some papers. I sat opposite her, and in between us was our family history.

She picked up a photo and gave it to me to look at. There was a man. He was sitting straight-backed at a table. He held a wooden paintbrush with a soft curved black tip; it looked like he was doing very delicate work. Around him were four small pots of ink. He had ears like Ba's. He must be Ye Ye, my grandfather. Ba must have been really upset with Ye Ye, because he didn't even have any photos of him at home; I'd certainly never seen one. I liked seeing my grandfather for the first time. Ye Ye had neat hair combed to one side, and I could tell he was very good at concentrating. On the paper in front of him, there were big black brushstrokes. I wondered what he was drawing.

Nai Nai showed me photo of her and Ye Ye with a little baby. "Ba?" I asked. Nai Nai nodded and smiled. Another one was of Nai Nai and Ye Ye: they were standing in front of a shop counter. There were rows and rows of jars full of small things, perhaps dried fruits. And there was a black and white one of her holding a stick with a silver plate on one end and a weight on the other. That must have been what she used to weigh things. No wonder she was so good with numbers; she'd had to measure and weigh things every day. Then there was a close-up of Ye Ye—he was smiling directly into the camera, and young Ba was poking his head around Ye Ye's shoulder. They looked happy.

She took the photo and held it up in front of her face and kissed it. She then pressed it to her chest and swayed from side to side. Her eyelids slowly closed. She looked like a little girl who was rocking a doll.

I didn't want to disturb her, so I gently pulled some of the other papers toward me that she had put out. They were drawings. Well, not drawings like what I did. They were paintings. Some with those big black brushstrokes I'd seen in the picture, and some were more detailed and done in color. Fish swam in small blue ponds; birds flew in cloudy skies. Red suns rose above black mountains. Nai Nai had been trying to show me that Ye Ye was an artist too. I was just like him! Ba had always said there was math in our blood, but he never mentioned that there was art, too—that I was the grandson of an artist. I wished he had told me more about Ye Ye and why he had stopped speaking to him.

When I looked up, Nai Nai was crying. I put down the painting I was holding, then slid across the floor. I patted her arm. She wiped her face on her sleeve. I checked for snot, but it was clean.

"Are you all right, Nai Nai?" I asked. I knew I wasn't going to really understand what she would say to me, but when someone was sad, you just knew. Mr. Heathfield said it doesn't take a rocket scientist to know such things, which I thought was strange, since rocket scientists probably only know about rockets and science. Did they know how to do a 360 on a scooter or how to make dim sum? I definitely wasn't a rocket scientist, but I knew Nai Nai was sad inside. Sometimes I'm sad too. But I didn't have anyone to tell until now. My sadness must have triggered her sadness, since she was trying to show me something important to her.

"Ye Ye? He's very hao, hao." I felt silly saying "good, good," but I didn't know the right words. He wasn't actually good, was he? He was actually dead. But I wished I knew how to tell her that he looked like a nice guy. She nodded and rubbed her finger over his face.

Nai Nai started humming a tune. She had put the framed photo of Ye Ye back in the envelope. Poor Nai Nai, she had lost a lot of people. I was so glad she had Mrs. Cruikshanks and, well, us. She needed to get out of the apartment and see her friend. She deserved to play bingo and I didn't care what my parents said; I was going to take her there again tomorrow. What they didn't know wouldn't hurt them, as Mrs. Cruikshanks had said.

# CHAPTER 21

## Eyes Down

**I'd become an expert in the white lie.** First to Ravi and then with my parents. But it was for the greater good. Bingo was where Nai Nai needed to be. I might not have any friends right now, but I was determined for Nai Nai to still have fun.

Nai Nai and I were now pros at sneaking out of the takeaway. When we arrived at the community center for bingo, Enid Blue Hair and her special friends were ready with their markers lined up in neat rows. I saw them glancing at Nai Nai as she began to give some people who were sitting by themselves free fruit. Enid's crew were shaking their heads, and their grumbles were low, but it was clear they weren't okay with Nai Nai being her friendly self.

Suddenly a familiar voice boomed over the airways. It

was Mrs. Cruikshanks; her Scottish accent was unmistakable. "A wee reminder that bingo is for everyone. Yes, everyone. And I mean black, white, brown, yellow, and purple. And while we're on that note—there are no reserved seats in bingo either. Yes, I'm talking about you, Enid O'Grady." Some people tutted, while others laughed and nodded. Nai Nai didn't know what the heck was going on; she just saw Mrs. Cruikshanks onstage and waved to her with a banana in her hand.

In the background we heard a scuffle and a man's voice: "Give me that microphone, Nellie. You're not supposed to be up here."

"Calm yerself down, Tommy. It was a public broadcasting announcement."

"Now!" Tommy said.

Mrs. Cruikshanks got off the stage and was a bit wobbly when she made her way over to us. "You're here, Danny! Come on quick, let's get ready." She swung Nai Nai's arm into her own and whisked us off to three empty seats in the middle of the bingo hall. I felt odd being the only boy there.

"I'm going to stay and watch if that's all right," I said to Mrs. Cruikshanks.

"Of course, Danny, loads of people bring their caregivers or relatives. You can get some punch if you want. Tell them I sent you."

I jogged off to get a quick cup of juice, then raced back and drank it at Nai Nai's table. The air felt electrified as we waited for the bingo to start. Even the hairs on my arms were standing on end. Nai Nai was focused. I looked at her eyes: they were staring forward. She was nodding her head as if it were revving her engine. She reminded me of an athlete warming up before a big race. Beside her she'd brought a large green plastic bowl the size of a basin, and had already plonked in there were lychees, cherries, and a kiwi. She'd given Mrs. Cruikshanks a plastic bag full of satsumas and in return Mrs. Cruikshanks had spread out a bag of Murray Mints between the two of them. She threw me one.

"Get yer chops around that, Danny . . ." She looked at the clock. "What's keeping them? It's supposed to be time."

"Eyes down," Tommy announced. He was a large man with a belly that looked like he was having six babies. His red-rimmed glasses looked like they might slip from his nose at any moment. I bet he felt like a king high up there onstage. He controlled the magic. He was master of the bobbling balls. He was the bingo god. All these people were his worshippers and I was a curious onlooker. I sucked on my Murray Mint and watched with anticipation.

"Ready?" asked Mrs. Cruikshanks. She held up two thumbs to Nai Nai, who responded with her own two upright thumbs. Then Mrs. Cruikshanks swung around to me.

"You ready to see yer nan win?" Mrs. Cruikshanks said. I nodded. My belly was fluttering around.

Then it started.

The machine was whirling; the balls were jostling one another like people looking for a bargain during a sale. I couldn't take my eyes off them. In that glass tank was the promise of a win—a token here, a prize there. Anyone could win. It was luck and skill. Mrs. Cruikshanks was right: you could be any kind of human and still win at bingo. It was a game of equals. No wonder Nai Nai loved it. She was in her element.

A green ball was sucked up the tube.

"And the first ball is two fat ladies . . . eighty-eight." The number eighty-eight lit up on the screen. Nai Nai stamped her card.

"Ba ba . . . hao, hao." She nodded. I could see a good start was making her feel confident. Eights were very lucky in Chinese culture.

"Is she singing 'Baa, Baa, Black Sheep'?" asked Mrs. Cruikshanks, not looking at me, her marker pen poised to go.

"No . . . 'ba' means 'eight.' It's very lucky for her."

"But I thought 'baa baa' meant 'dad'?"

"Yes, well, it does. But it's a different tone. It's complicated to explain."

"Too bloody right it's complicated. You Chinese come here, speaking your complex language and then learning ours, which is also one of the hardest to learn. No wonder you're all geniuses—you ought to be commended."

"We're not all geniuses; that's a myth. And I was born here; I didn't come from anywhere but the hospital," I said, but she wasn't listening.

"Oh yes! I got that one!" She blotted out another number.

This went on for some time. In between calls, Nai Nai would grab a cherry or lychee, discard the shell or stem, and suck on it. She'd roll it around her mouth, sometimes storing it in her cheek if she had to concentrate hard.

Looking over at her board, I could see one of her rows was almost complete.

Her foot nearest to me was tapping the floor. She was close and she knew it.

She needed fifty-six.

"Come on, twenty-seven . . . Nellie will be very happy if you show your face," Mrs. Cruikshanks said.

I squirmed and crossed my legs. Now was not a good time to need the bathroom; it was the most exciting part! Nope, I definitely had to go. I got up and quickly ran to the bathroom, which was near the exit.

As I ran back into the hall, I was expecting to see some lucky person onstage collecting a prize. Instead there was a commotion. Loads of people were gathered in a bunch near the middle of the hall where our seats were. I couldn't get down the aisles; they were full of people.

"What's happened?" I asked as I jostled over an old gentleman's walker.

"Some old lady called out 'bingo,' but then I think it was too much and she collapsed."

"I think it was that Chinese woman . . ." a voice said.

Nai Nai?

I pushed my way through the crowd.

"I need to get through!" I shouted. "My grandmother! Let me through."

When I made it past everyone in my way, it was clear that Nai Nai's chair was empty.

Where was Nai Nai?

Was it her?

Had she died?

This was all my fault. I had encouraged her to come here. I made it to the front of the crowd and saw Nai Nai. She was kneeling on the floor. She didn't look ill—just sad. She was holding Mrs. Cruikshanks's hand. It was Mrs. Cruikshanks who was lying on the floor; her face was very pale and her eyes were closed. Nai Nai was chatting away to her. I could see Mrs. Cruikshank's cardigan going up and down, so I knew she was still alive. She was gripping her bingo card in one hand, and a marker in the other.

"I'm calling 911! Be quiet, all of you!" shouted Linda, the manager.

I bent down and put my hand on Nai Nai's back. She turned to face me; her eyes were wet.

"Dan Dan," she said. "Ah-ya. Nellie." She held her hand out to me and I gently pulled as she rose from the floor. She put her arm around my middle and gave it a squeeze. I was so happy it wasn't Nai Nai down there. Not only because I would be in the worst trouble in history, but also because I was starting to like her. And—dare I say it?—I even loved her. When that voice said they thought it was the "Chinese woman," I'd almost cried. But poor Mrs. Cruikshanks. I hadn't seen anyone ill like that before. Nai Nai kept her eyes on her friend.

Tommy, the bingo caller, was standing onstage with his microphone. "Everyone stop being nosy. Nellie needs some space!" his voice boomed through the speakers.

"The ambulance is coming. We'd be very grateful if you could all make your way outside. Someone please bring Nellie's bag here," Linda said, her phone still to her ear.

"This is all very inconvenient," said Enid.

I felt my palms bunch up and I was about to say something, but then the exit doors burst open and two paramedics arrived.

Linda was standing on tiptoe to see them over the heads of the crowd. "Over here!" She waved at them.

"Come on, Enid. Let's go to the café and have a cup of tea," her husband said. "We'll come tomorrow for the Grand Bingo Tournament. I'm sure it'll all be back to normal by then."

Typical: all Enid and her husband were thinking about were themselves, not Mrs. Cruikshanks and how ill she was. The paramedics were quick to check her vitals. Two more paramedics wheeled in more equipment and a stretcher. They gently lifted her onto it and tucked her in, pulling up the metal bars on the sides. One paramedic covered her face in a clear plastic mask attached to an oxygen tank. Tommy had grabbed Mrs. Cruikshanks's bag from the table and, as the stretcher passed, carefully put it under the thick white blanket.

Nai Nai moved back to where we had been sitting. Loads of Mrs. Cruikshanks's stuff was still on the table; Tommy had forgotten all of her favorite things. Her picture of Jesus, her cat cushion, and her special markers were still lying there with some mints, a half-eaten tea cake and the bag of satsumas Nai Nai had bought for her. Nai Nai picked up my backpack from the back of her chair and began to put Mrs. Cruikshanks's things inside, but not the tea cake. Her own bag was full to the brim with fruit. Nai Nai and I headed out of the exit doors, being carried along like flotsam on a sea of bingo regulars.

When we got outside, Nai Nai kept pointing at the ambulance as it sped off around the corner. Her eyes were welling up.

A man standing next to me tapped me on the shoulder. "Your laces are undone," he said, pointing to my sneakers.

"Thanks," I replied, and bent down to tie them. I glanced up and saw Nai Nai moving away from me. "Nai Nai, wait a minute," I said, finishing the knot. I stood up and searched for Nai Nai in the crowd but couldn't see her. She was gone.

I looked left and right. Her familiar headband and massive bag were nowhere to be seen. I couldn't believe it. I'd lost my nai nai.

# CHAPTER 22

## Friends Reunited

**Nai Nai didn't know many places apart from home, school, the Global Mini-Mart, and the bingo hall.** She couldn't speak English well enough to make her way to the hospital, could she? How could I have been so silly as to have lost my gran? If my parents found out I was not with her, I'd be in massive trouble.

*Think, Danny, think!* I told myself, but instead my mind was as blank as a newly wiped whiteboard. I wished Ravi were there. He would know what to do. *That's it*, I thought. *Ravi!*

I ran all the way to Ravi's house from the Longdale Community Center. I was sweating and had a pain in my side by the time I arrived. I rang the doorbell and then put my hands on my thighs to catch my breath. My face was dripping with sweat. I looked up and saw the front room curtain twitch.

Then the front door opened and Ravi slid out; he already had his jacket on. I could hear Ravi's sisters arguing and Vishal crying—Ravi's mom was shouting.

"Ravi . . . look . . . I wanted to say . . ." My heartbeat was thumping in my chest and my hands were clammy. I didn't know if it was due to the running or because I was scared that he wouldn't accept my apology.

"Tell me in a minute. I need to get out of this house, man. It's so loud in there, I can't think. Let's go." He zipped up his jacket and shut the front door. We walked down his driveway and around the hedge.

"Ravi, I wanted first to say . . ." I had to slow down my words to breathe.

"Why did you run here? Been playing with your new best friends? Blasters and all that?"

"No . . . no, you were right. They weren't cool at all. I wanted to say . . . I'm sorry."

"All right . . ." Ravi looked at the pavement. Then he looked at me. "I'm sorry too."

"Truce?" I asked.

"Definitely. I didn't mean to tell Tia that you shared a bunk bed with your gran. Then I was going to tell you after school, but you were with Carter."

"Well, I was angry at you . . . And I wanted to play Blasters . . ." Ravi hadn't done it on purpose to make me look bad. I should have just asked him about it straightaway instead of thinking he was being a bad friend.

"How was it, then?" he asked.

"Well . . . let's just say that birds of a feather really do flock together. It was like hanging out with a bunch of dodos. You were right. Carter is just as bad as the other two. And he didn't care about the mutants in my comics or finger jousting."

"Man, he's missing out. Your comics are so funny," Ravi said. It made me feel all warm and fuzzy.

"How about a finger joust to make up officially?" I asked, raising my eyebrows hopefully.

"Sure." Ravi grinned and got his index finger out, and we circled each other like old times, trying to jab each other in the side. His arms were much longer than mine and he jabbed me in the ribs.

"Ow!" I cackled. "Haven't lost it, Sir Ravi." It was good to see him. I didn't have to pretend to be someone else with Ravi.

"Nope! Still got it. Anyway, how has your spring break been so far?" Ravi said as we got to the bottom of his road.

"That's why I'm here actually . . . It's been wild." My breathing was going back to normal.

"Tell me about it. School holidays with my family have made me loopy. You don't look like yourself—what's up?"

"Well, Nai Nai and I were at bingo and Mrs. Cruikshanks—she's a customer but also Nai Nai's only friend—she collapsed when I was in the bathroom." I couldn't get the words out fast enough. It had all happened too quickly.

"Did she collapse because you stank up the place?" He grinned and hit my arm—typical Ravi.

"No, man, it was serious, like, she fell down. Maybe a stroke or something. It was really scary, since I thought it was my nai nai at first. They took her off in an ambulance. But then Nai Nai vanished right after. My parents told me not to take her to bingo, but I did, and now she's gone. I know I've been awful, but I need your help, Rav. I don't know what to do!"

"First, I think you need to make it up to me big-time, Danny Chung."

"I thought you'd accepted my apology."

"I did, but I'm gonna milk it. Down on your knee like a plebeian asking a feudal lord for mercy."

"All right. I, Danny Chung of the Lucky Dragon takeaway, hereby offer my sincerest apology to my very best friend, Ravi Sebastian Dalal, otherwise known as Sir Ravi of Longdale. I was a total moron for lying to you to hang out with Carter. Are we cool?"

"Sure. Okay. You can get up now," Ravi said, smiling. He held out his fist for me to bump.

"I'm so glad we're together again!" I said.

"Me too," he said.

With Sir Ravi by my side, I felt more confident about sorting out my mess.

"It's all right. Let's go find your gran," Ravi said. "Let's head back to your place and see if she just went home. Then, if she's not there, we can check the hospital."

I knew he would help me out. And just like that—order was restored. Well, with me and Ravi, anyway.

When Ravi and I arrived back at the takeaway, there was no sign of Nai Nai. I had hoped she would be sitting at the dining room table spitting out seeds. Her boots weren't at the bottom of the stairs, and it was eerily quiet—no humming, no babbling, nothing. Just then, the kitchen door opened, and Ba came out.

"Hi, Ravi, it's been ages," he said. I'd hoped he and Ma were out, but no such luck.

The front door jangled and then Ma came in with her arms full of shopping bags, and behind her was Auntie Yee, who wouldn't look at me; her arms were also full of bags. I wasn't expecting to see Auntie Yee after the "incident." But here she was, still poking her nose in.

"Oh, it's you. Your mother kindly offered to buy me a new bag to apologize for your behavior last time I was here. Amelia is still upset about what you said about her and she didn't want to come this time." *Lucky Amelia,* I thought.

"Danny, where is Nai Nai? I got a new pair of slippers for her on sale," asked Ma, looking around.

"Ma . . . Ba," I said, "I have to tell you something."

"Nai Nai's boots aren't here. Where is she?" Ma continued.

I looked at Ravi and he nodded.

"I'm sorry! I took Nai Nai to bingo, but then the ambulance came . . ."

"Ambulance?" both of my parents said together. Three sets of adult eyes homed in on me. Ba put his hands on his hips.

"Bingo again? Such a preposterous pastime, so uncultured," Auntie Yee said. "I warned you. Now she has had a heart attack."

"No, Nai Nai hasn't had a heart attack. Mrs. Cruikshanks has, or maybe a stroke?" I added.

"Su Lin, this is exactly—" Auntie Yee began.

"Clarissa, please let Danny speak," Ma said curtly.

"Yes, Clarissa, please be quiet. It's about my mother," Ba said. Auntie Yee looked shocked that he had told her to pipe down. "Well, Danny? What happened?" Ba asked.

"I've lost her. She was there one minute, then gone the next."

There was a sharp intake of breath from all three grown-ups in the room.

"Lost her? Lost my mother?" Ba repeated.

"I know, I'm the worst grandson in the world . . . but . . . let me make this right. I'm sure I can find her. I owe you all that much."

"Yes, Mr. and Mrs. Chung. We know this neighborhood like the back of our hands. I'm sure we can find her," said Ravi. "We can make a list of all of the places that Ant Gran . . . I mean, Danny's gran would know. She can't have gone that far; Longdale is not that big."

"Terrible idea," Auntie Yee proclaimed.

"It is not," I said. "I've taken her around this whole spring break and I'm the one who lost her. I have to be the one who finds her. Plus, the takeaway opens soon, so you and Ba have to be here." I had to convince them to let me do this alone. It was my fault that Nai Nai was missing.

"I think it's a mistake, but what do I know?" said Auntie Yee, looking at her nails.

"No, I think Danny's right," Ma countered. "As long as you stay together, okay?" Ravi and I nodded. "You're right: we do have to be here. There's a big order coming in at six tonight and we open in forty-five minutes. I don't have time to go look for her myself and then be back to do the counter." Ma looked to Ba, who was still thinking.

Ba put his hand on my shoulder, then nodded. "All right. Danny, I'm trusting you can handle this and find your nai nai before it gets dark. She knows her way around in the daylight, but things look different at night." There was no Chinese Way lecture from Ba. What was going on? There'd been fewer of them since Nai Nai moved in.

Auntie Yee looked at me and Ravi and made a face. "I'd call the police if I were you, Su Lin. She's vulnerable," she said, rummaging in her bag. She pulled out her phone. "I would try to find her myself, but I need to get back to Amelia. She's got piano practice this evening. Adrian is with her now, helping her with her math project."

But something had changed. My mom wasn't taking the bait this time. "No, Clarissa, we trust Danny. He says he'll find her, and we have to give him that chance." She smiled at me.

"Yes, go bring my mother back home," Ba said. With that, he turned and walked into the kitchen.

Ma grabbed two bags of shrimp crackers and handed them to me and Ravi. "Put these in your bag; you'll be missing dinner."

My bag. Where was my bag?

"What's wrong?" Ravi asked. "What's the matter? Why do you look like a zombie?"

"Nai Nai has my backpack. And my sketchbook is in it . . ."

Ravi stared at me with wide eyes. He knew what she'd find if she opened the sketchbook.

I grabbed his jacket sleeve. "She's going to see my Ant Gran, Supervillain, comic." Ant Gran swallowed by a lion mutated with a poodle. Ant Gran flung into a black hole. Ant Gran being squished by a giant clown shoe with menacing eyes. Ant Gran catapulted into the sky by a catapult and eaten by the Druckon. Quack.

That last one was Ravi's idea.

I had to find Nai Nai before she looked at my comics.

I felt like I was going to throw up.

# CHAPTER 23

## Lost and Found

**We ran to the hospital's ER and Ravi told the receptionist that he was a friend of Mrs. Cruikshanks's family.** We described her and they told us which area she was in. A nurse walked us down the middle of the ER; cubicles flanked each side.

"Visiting finishes in fifteen minutes, though, for dinner-time," the nurse said.

"What does she look like?" Ravi whispered.

"Old white Scottish lady with curly gray hair, a few whiskers, thick brown glasses . . ." I recounted. "Maybe about ninety-five?"

"I can hear you, Danny! You cheeky blighter. I'm not ninety-five! I'm in here!" Mrs. Cruikshanks's voice boomed from behind a curtain.

We jogged over to the cubicle and pulled the orange curtain aside. Mrs. Cruikshanks was strapped to a machine and she had tubes going into her nose.

"Are you okay, Mrs. Cruikshanks?" I said.

"I've been better. I had a mini-stroke, they said. I prefer mini pretzels! Flippin' bingo was nearly the end of me." She waved her hand at Ravi. "Hello, Danny's pal. I've had a little problem with my blood flow to my brain . . . Thankfully Him up above had other ideas; it was not my day to go meet my Maker, no sir."

"Look," said Ravi as he bent down to pick up my backpack from the floor. It was open.

"Your wee nan brought me my Lord and my comfy cushion." Her cat cushion was propping up her back.

"Yes, about her. Do you know where she might have gone?"

"She's upset, Danny. She found these." Mrs. Cruikshanks picked up my sketchbook from the side table. "Not very nice, are they? You've broken her heart."

My chest felt tight. "I'm sorry that happened. I really am. I didn't mean to hurt Nai Nai's feelings," I said, and I meant it. I'd gotten really good at hurting people lately. It made me feel terrible.

Ravi looked at me. His eyes grazed the ground. He'd written some of the speech bubbles.

"It wasn't just Danny—it was me too. We didn't mean any harm. I'm sorry too."

"Well, it has hurt her . . . hurt her a lot. I am disappointed in you, Danny. I thought you were a good 'un."

"I know . . . I was wrong to do these. Do you know where she is?"

"I don't. All I know is that she left here with tears in her eyes. Tears. I'll not be surprised if she's lost her winning mojo after this. The Grand Prize is on tomorrow, and I was sure she was going to win it. Haven't seen someone as fast as her in years." Mrs. Cruikshanks looked very pale. "Anyway, go and tell one of the nurses I want a cup of tea, will ya?"

We left the hospital with my backpack and a leaflet about the Grand Prize Tournament that Mrs. Cruikshanks had given us.

"Where to next?" Ravi asked.

"She loves fruit. Maybe she bought some from Mr. Potempa."

We ran down the alleyway that led to the main street where Mr. Potempa's fruit and vegetable displays brightened up the pavement.

"Hi, Mr. Potempa. I was wondering if my grandma had been in here to buy any fruit today."

"Yes, Danny, she did come in earlier—about four, I think. She bought tons of produce. Enough for two whole weeks, by my calculations. Is she having bowel issues again?"

"No . . . no . . . I don't know. Look, we need to find her."

"Did she say where she was going?" interrupted Ravi.

"Not in any language I ever learned," Mr. Potempa said, chuckling.

"But did she look okay?"

Mr. Potempa stood up and adjusted some packages on the counter. "Danny . . . I am not in the business of psychological evaluation, my friend. She looked like she needed some fruit to sweeten her up, yes, but then, I don't like to get involved in my customers' personal lives. You know how it is. Small talk, yes; large talk, no. I'm too busy running a business for large talk."

Ravi had wandered toward the chocolate rack.

"She got out her bus pass and was waving toward the street," said Mr. Potempa. "I think she was asking me where the nearest bus stop was. The closest bus to here is the Inner Circle one."

"Okay . . . she got herself to the hospital, so where is she trying to get to now?" I wondered.

"Okay, thanks, Mr. Potempa. What time was that?" asked Ravi.

"About twenty past four . . . I hope you find her . . . And, Danny . . ."

"Yes?"

"She bought a bunch of plums and all of my lychees. A whole bag." He waved goodbye as we left his store.

Ravi and I started to walk down the main street in the hope of finding her.

"She can't be far. I mean, a whole bag of lychees is going to be heavy," I said.

The main street was still busy despite the shops nearing closing time. The light was beginning to fade. Ravi was really getting into the role of granny finder. He was going from one person to the next, asking in his most serious voice: "Chinese granny! Has anyone seen a Chinese granny?" He'd taken to the quest quite well.

I gently patted him on the arm and asked, "Ravi, do you think that people will take you seriously if you're shouting that?"

"I dunno, I thought it might help."

"Okay, I guess it's better than not saying anything."

I joined in too.

"Chinese granny missing! Reward of free shrimp crackers! But don't tell my parents! Free food in exchange for Chinese granny. Again . . . don't tell my parents." We were like ye olde English town criers with no bell.

After five minutes of asking about possible sightings, we decided to give up on that tactic, as our throats were beginning to hurt. We trudged around for ages, peering into the row of thrift shops that lay back from the main road. I had to stop Ravi from browsing the piles of old DVDs that they put in boxes outside the windows. We jogged toward the park. My feet were aching, and time was running out.

"I think I better go home and tell my parents that I can't find her," I said, feeling defeated. Where would an old Chinese lady with a bag full of lychees go on a Friday evening if she wanted to be alone? I had no idea. My belly made a gurgling sound.

"Maybe we would be able to think more clearly if we had something to eat," said Ravi. "I'm kinda hungry now, and from the sounds of it, so are you. Could we have a teeny tiny break from the search?"

"All right, but only for a short while," I replied.

We stood outside Lickin' Chicken.

"I'll get us some fries and a drink," Ravi said.

I passed him a couple of pounds. "Good idea. Thanks." I looked at all the people passing by. Nai Nai wasn't anywhere.

Ravi went in and soon appeared with a cone of fries and two soda cans protruding out of his jacket pockets. We sat down on a bench and began to eat.

"Hey, thanks for coming," I said, wiping my fingers on my jeans.

"It's all right," Ravi said. "It's been quite the adventure and so not boring or loud, like my house."

I grunted and started bobbing my head to one side, trying to say *Look over there* without bringing attention to myself.

"Are you okay, Danny? Why are you doing that with your head? Do you want more fries?" Ravi said, offering me the cone.

"No . . . it's Carter," I whispered. "He's . . . over there."

Ravi turned and saw Carter, Mitchell, and Jay Jay heading toward us, Blaster guns in hand across their chests. Carter was wearing a navy baseball cap. As he loomed closer, I could see it said *TAKE NO PRISONERS* on it.

Ravi crumpled the cone up. He took the soda can from my hand and went to drop it in the recycling bin a few feet away. I hoped he would be back before Carter reached us.

"Well, well, well . . . if it isn't the Danny who loves his granny," said Mitchell. It was his attempt at being a poet.

Ravi returned from the bin, his thumbs hooked into his jacket pockets. His face looked odd.

"Yeah," said Jay Jay.

"Carter, guys . . . this is not a great time. Look, I'm sorry I—" I began.

"Chung, you're gonna get it," said Mitchell, pointing his Blaster at my face. Carter laughed.

I really hoped Ravi had his running shoes on. We stood close to each other, our arms touching.

"Boys, boys. No need for that. Danny can't help it if he's poor and has to share a room with his gran. He can't help it that he lives in an apartment. Remember, Danny, I told you—make an enemy of me and that's it," Carter said, drops of spittle hitting my face.

"Loads of people live in apartments," said Ravi. "There's nothing wrong with Danny's apartment."

"It's okay, Ravi," I said, patting his arm. "Carter . . ." I didn't know what was going to come out of my mouth.

"Yes, Danny?" he asked.

"Erm . . . well, you see the thing is . . . I couldn't have helped you even if I had wanted to. I'm no good at math."

"I don't believe you," Carter said. He held his free hand up as if to say, *Enough talking*. Slowly, he pointed his Blaster at me.

"Danny, be prepared to be pelted," Mitchell said. "You have five seconds. Then it's your turn." He looked at Ravi.

Behind him I could see a double-decker bus moving toward us. I glanced at the top windows. I couldn't believe my eyes. I blinked and looked harder. It couldn't be . . . It was Nai Nai. She was on the top deck, right at the front!

"Excuse me, Carter, but I've got to get THAT bus." I pointed to the Inner Circle bus, which basically went around and around in a big loop.

"You ain't going anywhere," said Mitchell.

"Ravi, she's on the bus," I whispered.

The bus was almost near the bus stop behind Carter and his gang. I'd have to run about five meters to catch it. It was going to be tricky getting past them, but we had to do it, as Nai Nai was just going to end up going around in another circle and that was going to be my fault too. We'd have to wait another half an hour for the bus to come around again.

"Let us pass, Carter," I said.

"You're free to go," he replied. His smirk made me want to draw him as my next evil villain.

"Get ready," whispered Ravi.

*Ready for what?*

*To run?*

*To be blasted in the face by Carter and his gang?*

I had no clue what Ravi was talking about.

"One, two, three . . . go!" Ravi ran toward the three boys with his arms outstretched. He started to shriek like a banshee. "Cooookkkkkkcuuuuuu!!!!" He started to finger joust them. They didn't know what was going on. Carter's eyes widened. They'd never seen Ravi like this. I'd never seen Ravi like this. Watching Vishal's karate lessons had paid off! Ravi quickly brandished his can of soda, shaking it hard. As he ran toward them, he shouted to me, "Get on the bus!" His soda grenade exploded all over the boys. They didn't know what had hit them! It was wet and cherry-flavored. Sir Ravi of Longdale—my hero! I'd never seen him stand up to them before.

I sprinted as hard as I could. I passed the four of them and waved at the driver as he was about to shut the doors. He pushed a button and they opened for me. I dragged myself on. My chest was hurting so bad, like a massive boot had kicked me there. I fished in my pocket for some coins and dropped them into the fare box. Turning to see what was happening outside, I saw Ravi running away from the bus, waving at me. Then he put his two thumbs up as he weaved through people on the main street.

Holding on tight to the banister, I made my way upstairs to face Nai Nai.

# CHAPTER 24

## Ant Gran, Superhero!

**Nai Nai looked very small sitting on the front seat.** Even smaller than usual. Next to her was a large plastic bag with lychee branches sticking out. She didn't turn. She just stared forward as I sat in the other seat at the front of the bus. Breathing as deeply as I could to calm myself down, I placed my backpack on the floor at our feet.

"Nai Nai, I'm sorry," I said. She didn't move. Her eyes remained forward. "Nai Nai, I'm sorry I drew those pictures of you." Still nothing. "It's true, I was angry at first that I had to share my bedroom with you. It's not easy being eleven. And I . . . well, I know I complain about my chores and stuff. But school is hard when all the others look like they are having more fun than you . . . I mean, me."

Thinking about how she must have felt made me tear up a little. My eyes were starting to get wet.

"Nai Nai, I'm really sorry!" I leaned over toward her, wrapped my arms around her, and laid my head on her shoulder. She patted my back. I didn't mean to make her cardigan wet. I wiped my snot off her with my sleeve.

"Hao. Hao. Dan Dan." She was talking to me. She leaned over and gently took my backpack from the floor. She pulled out my sketchbook and flicked it to a drawing of Ant Gran being tossed into the jaws of the Druckon.

I took the book and ripped out those pages, tearing them to pieces.

She turned to me; the whites of her eyes were red. She wiped her nose on a hanky.

I began to scribble. I was working so fast, but I knew exactly what I wanted to draw. A new Nai Nai comic strip—one that she would be proud of. When I was finished, I laid it in her lap.

I pointed to where I had sketched her with a cape and a massive *8* on her chest.

Although I wasn't sure she would appreciate me drawing her with her flowery underwear on the outside of her tights, she didn't seem to mind. She stared at it. It felt like ages before she turned to me.

"Nai Nai ai Dan Dan," she said. *Love.* She still loved me even though I'd been the worst grandson ever, by writing mean

things about her and then trying to ditch her at bingo so I
could have fun.

"I love you too, Nai Nai. I have been an idiot." I patted my
chest. "Idiot."

She nodded. At least we agreed on something. I remembered we needed to get off the bus and I knew what would do
it. I handed her the leaflet Mrs. Cruikshanks had given me.

"Your friend Mrs. Cruikshanks is okay. She gave me this.
Tomorrow you want to go to bingo?"

She scanned the leaflet and even though I knew she
couldn't read the words, she recognized the numbers for a lot

of money. She sprang up. "Hao-si!" "House"—she understood. She grabbed her fruit bag and nudged me out of the way. Then she took my hand and pulled me down the stairs. The bell rang and we got off the bus.

The bus had gone around in a circle and come back to the main street, so once we'd gotten off, we saw Ravi running out of a bush next to the bus stop.

"I . . . I . . . held them off as long as I could," he panted. His body was bent over, his hands resting on his thighs.

"Are you all right?" I asked.

"No," he managed to say. "Stitch, ahhh." He stood up and put his hand on the side of his rib cage.

Nai Nai opened her handbag and rummaged around. She pulled out a small jar.

"Tiger Balm," I said.

She took Ravi's hand and splotched a dollop on his finger.

"Rub that into your side. It should help with the pain," I said.

Ravi lifted his shirt and rubbed it in.

"Hot, hot," he said. "No, it's actually feeling better." He bowed to Nai Nai like she was the queen.

Just then Carter and crew sprang out of the bushes, Blasters at the ready.

"Well, well, well," said Carter. He was a little out of breath, but the determination to inflict pain was still there.

"Look, he's got his little granny with him." Jay Jay laughed.

I moved in front of Nai Nai so that if they did start shooting, they wouldn't hit her.

"She's sooooo sweet, with her little bags and her woolly hat. She looks like an elf," Carter said.

"Don't you talk about my nai nai like that," I said.

"What you gonna do, nana's boy?" taunted Mitchell.

"You're so unfortunate, Danny. I could have made you into one of the coolest boys in the class. Instead you hang out with these two losers," Carter said, aiming his gun at my chest. Mitchell was aiming at Nai Nai and Jay Jay at Ravi.

I leaned back into Nai Nai. Feeling out the plastic bag in her hand, I grabbed it and swung it toward the ground in front of us. Dropping down, I gathered a handful of lychees and started chucking them toward Carter. One hit him dead center on the nose. I quickly took aim and threw three more. They hit him in the forehead.

"OW! Ow! Get them!" he shouted to his cronies.

However, before Jay Jay or Mitchell could shoot, Nai Nai swooped forward and grabbed a bunch of the hard, spiky-skinned fruit and began lobbing them at Mitchell like a baseball pitcher. Her aim was magnificent. She hit him in all types of places, especially places that hurt boys. Ravi got in on the action, and soon the place was covered in brown and red shells. Some had cracked open, and the carnage that was white slime-balls littered the pavement.

Mitchell turned and ran away. Carter grabbed Jay Jay and ducked behind his smaller friend.

"Get off me, Carter! Let me go!" Jay Jay obviously didn't appreciate being used as a human shield. He wriggled and squirmed out of Carter's grip and followed in the direction that Mitchell had fled. One of them had left a Blaster on the ground in the commotion.

Ravi walked over to it and picked it up.

"Be a shame to leave it here," he said. He held it to his chest.

"HAO-SI!" Nai Nai said and picked up the bag of remaining lychees.

Nai Nai's eyes sparkled with excitement as we headed toward home. While she'd been going around and around on the Inner Circle bus by herself, she had eaten a lot of fruit. I could smell that she'd had plums, and the little *pumpety-pumps* her bottom made told me that she had enjoyed them immensely. It would have to be the last time I ever took Nai Nai to bingo, but it was worth it. Even if I was grounded for a month. I owed her this.

## CHAPTER 25

# Cyborg Devil Rebellion

**Today was the day!** The Grand Bingo Tournament was being held at the Longdale Community Center at the usual time of two p.m. Ravi had come over to offer moral support. He sat next to me on the sofa as we watched Nai Nai.

"Does she always walk up and down like that?" he asked, watching Nai Nai pace the living room carpet.

"Not normally," I said. Nai Nai kept looking at the clock.

"Did you absolutely promise your parents not to take her to bingo ever again?" Ravi asked.

"I did promise, but I guess it wasn't an 'absolute' promise," I said, trying to think of ways I could get out of it. Nai Nai had been there for me when I needed someone to help me and she'd stood up to Carter yesterday. She was part of our team now. It wasn't just me and Ravi anymore; Nai Nai was an honorary member of our gang and she deserved to go to that bingo tournament. I watched as she kept picking up the leaflet and then putting it down. She glanced at the clock on the wall as the time ticked closer and closer to the game beginning.

"We've got to take her," I said to Ravi. "We just need to get out of here without being noticed." I sat on the edge of the sofa and began scribbling a note to my parents. Just then, the living room door opened and Ma entered, followed by Auntie Yee and Amelia. Auntie Yee was wearing a lilac dress, and Amelia was in jeans and a gray sweater. It was the first time I had seen her looking different from her mother, no color coordination whatsoever! It was a Cyborg Devil rebellion.

I was still wary of her, though, so I slid the note down the side of the sofa into the cushions and motioned to Ravi with my eyes to hide the Grand Bingo Tournament leaflet that was on the coffee table. He started to do weird stretches like he had just gotten out of bed. Amelia frowned when she saw him. He did a side lunge and knocked the leaflet behind the coffee table and out of sight.

Amelia was sulking. "But do I have to stay here? Why can't I just stay at home with Daddy?"

"I told you, he's coming with me and we don't have room in the car for the new mirror if you are there too—we need to put down the back seat. I can't have a cracked mirror in my bedroom. It's bad luck."

"It's no problem," said Ma. "You are free to stay all afternoon if you like, Amelia."

"That won't be necessary, Su Lin. Just an hour will suffice," Auntie Yee said.

"We'll be quick," said Uncle Yee, who appeared behind them all.

"We'll pick up the new mirror, drop it off at home, and then come pick you up and take you to your Royal Birmingham Conservatoire audition," added Auntie Yee, "We'll be less than an hour."

Amelia sank into the sofa. The note was sticking up.

"Thank you, Su Lin," Auntie Yee said. "Please be mindful of Amelia's braces—no food that might get clogged up. Amelia, be ready at two on the dot, as we can't miss the appointment with the conservatoire. We've waited six months . . ."

I saw Amelia roll her eyes a little and turn her head away from her mother. "YOU'VE waited six months . . ." I heard Amelia mutter under her breath.

The Yees left and Ma held the door for them. "Okay, kids, you entertain yourselves. Help yourself to fruit. We have enough to feed a village. I've got to go into the kitchen. No fighting now, okay?" With that, she turned and left the room.

Ravi recognized Amelia from the Cyborg Devil pictures,

braces and all. "You must be Amelia. I've heard all about you."
He gave me a big grin.

"Hi," she said. There was no barb or sarcastic taunt. What
was wrong with her today? "And you must be the famous Ravi.
Danny mentions you all the time."

I felt a bit weird. Amelia had actually been listening to what
I was saying even when she looked like she was ignoring me. I
then watched in horror as she noticed the paper down the side
of the sofa. She plucked it out and began to read it. "'Dear Ba
and Ma, there is somewhere that I HAVE to take Nai Nai today.
It's really important. I'm sorry! I hope you will understand. P.S.
I promise not to lose her this time!' Where do you HAVE to take
your nai nai?" Amelia asked.

I felt my face get red. I wasn't sure if I could trust her—she
was probably just going to tell on us. But I had little choice. She
was here and knew our plan.

Nai Nai came over to me and gave me the leaflet for the
Grand Bingo Tournament that she'd picked up from the floor.
She tapped it. Then pointed at the clock.

"Hao-si?" she asked.

"Bingo?" Amelia figured out. "She wants to go to bingo?"

"She wants to go really bad," Ravi said.

"We have to take her," I said. "But are you going to tell on us?"

"I haven't decided," Amelia said, getting up from the sofa.
Great, our fate rested in the hands of Amelia Yee. She'd tell her

**207**

mom, who would tell my parents, and all the good stuff I'd done, like finding Nai Nai on the bus, would be for nothing.

Nai Nai looked at the clock on the wall. Then she came up to me and held my hand. "Nellie, Hao-si. Winner." She patted her chest. My heart exploded. She wanted to win for Mrs. Cruikshanks. Nai Nai was talking to me and I could understand her. She was so clever and quick.

"We have to take her to bingo," Ravi said. "It's her knight-errant quest. I can take her if you want me to."

"No, I have to go too. She and I are a team—the Lucky Dragons. I have to be there to support her, because Mrs. Cruikshanks is still in the hospital. Okay, let's go . . . but . . ." I turned to stare at Amelia. She would snitch on us for sure.

Amelia bit her lip. "You can go if you want; I won't tell on you. In fact . . . can I come?"

I couldn't believe it. Amelia Yee was being . . . nice?

She continued. "This spring break has been the worst. Extra piano lessons, working on the math presentation every night. I don't want to meet the mayor of Birmingham or ride in a limo. I don't want to audition at the conservatoire, because then I'll have to practice even more. I just want to do something fun for a change. I promise not to tell, but only if I can come too."

I suddenly felt really sorry for Amelia. Her mom was a

beast. And Amelia never talked about her friends, never mentioned anyone by name. At least I had my best friend, Ravi.

I looked at Ravi; he looked at me. We both looked at Nai Nai.

"Okay, we're all going. Amelia too."

Amelia smiled. She looked actually . . . dare I say it? Friendly.

"Nai Nai . . ." I said, turning to my gran. "Come on, we're going to bingo!"

I left the note I'd written in the middle of the coffee table. Nai Nai did a little hop and ran to get her bag, emptying the fruit bowl into it. Then we all tiptoed downstairs, put on our shoes, and silently left the apartment, one by one. We walked as fast as we could down the street.

Yes, I would be grounded for life if Ma and Ba knew I had disobeyed them for a third time. But this was bigger than Ma and Ba. It was for Nai Nai. It was Nai Nai's Chinese Way! Ma and Ba were always going on and on about trying our best and succeeding in life. This was Nai Nai's chance to succeed here in a strange new land.

# CHAPTER 26

## AND THE WINNER IS . . .

**When we arrived at bingo, nearly every seat was taken.** Everybody wanted to win the two thousand pounds in prize money. We walked around and scanned the room, looking for a good location to see the board. There was a seat next to Enid, right in the middle of the room, but she quickly put her cardigan on the chair as we neared her. Nai Nai smiled and I heard a faint sound. I think my gran farted as she passed by her nemesis.

"No way," said Ravi. We chuckled and clamped our hands over our mouths and then over our noses. My god, Nai Nai was lethal. Fruit bombs!

Amelia and Ravi helped Nai Nai find a place to sit near the far wall, and I left for a minute to buy her bingo cards and then returned to join them. Enid wasn't the only player to have an entourage. I helped Nai Nai take off her lucky red-and-gold dragon jacket and placed it on the back of her chair. Amelia arranged the cards neatly in front of her. And Ravi massaged Nai Nai's shoulders. She got out her markers and fruit supplies from her handbag and sat still with her hand poised. We'd only just made it in time.

The lights went down. The screen turned on and the bingo balls began bobbing. Tommy, the bingo caller, was sitting in his chair.

"Welcome, everyone, to the Grand Bingo Tournament. I've heard from the hospital, and Nellie is doing fine. We're sending you best wishes, Nellie!"

Many of the bingo players looked relieved.

"Today we have a prize of a whopping two thousand pounds for one lucky winner, kindly sponsored by Sausages R Us. The first and second runners-up will receive a year's supply of sausages. Vegetarian sausages are also available. Are you ready?"

"Yes!" yelled the room.

"Get on with it!" shouted one of Enid's gang.

"Then it's eyes down!" Tommy began.

It was like being in a place where magic happened but you weren't in on the trick. You either had the numbers or you didn't. You either got there fast or you didn't. It was like this was Nai Nai's time, because it WAS her time. This was the most exciting day I'd ever had in my entire life! I held my breath as I watched Nai Nai go to work.

Her hand-eye coordination was impressive. She was concentrating hard but managed to still suck on some lychees. Her marker was blotting out numbers as soon as they were called. The numbers came thick and fast from the popping tube. The caller was eagle-eyed, checking to make sure he had the ball the right way around.

*Pop! Pop! Pop!*

The machine spat up the rainbow balls, one by one. The lights on the screen lit up as each ball was called. Furious hands, wrinkled hands, determined hands all over the bingo hall . . . battering the cards, covering them in pen-splotch measles. Nai Nai was on fire.

*Bam! Bam! Bam!* went her marker pen in pretty red.

I peered around the room in anticipation of someone else calling out "House." The Grand Prize would be gone just like that. I started to jog back and forth. I was the one who had ants in his pants now.

"God, this is so exciting!" squealed Amelia, hands to her mouth. This time she wasn't covering her braces; she was biting her fingers in excitement.

"It's like watching a master at work," said Ravi.

Then I saw them. Ba and Ma's heads passed the window outside. They must have gotten the note I'd left. Now they would be able to see how brilliant Nai Nai was at bingo. I was kinda glad to see them here, because she was so close now. Behind them trailed Auntie and Uncle Yee. What were they doing here? They couldn't come in now. It would be a disaster if they caused a ruckus. Nai Nai was nearly there.

"Look!" I pointed to the window. Amelia and Ravi turned. "What should we do?" I said, panicking. "Come on, let's block the doors."

We ran over and held the handles. Linda, the manager, was looking at us funny. She was starting to come over. Ba and Ma's heads appeared on the other side of the door as they looked through the window. Then Auntie Yee scrambled to the other door. She was fuming and pointing. We couldn't hear what she was saying, but it was way past two. Amelia had missed her audition at the conservatoire.

"You two, hold the doors. I need to check on Nai Nai!" I ran back to where my little gran was working hard. Her bingo cards were nearly full. It was excruciating. Nai Nai kept sucking on her lychees and, *pow*, the seeds went into the bin without her moving her head. She had perfected the side spit.

She only needed number eight now. Come on, lucky eight!

Linda had asked Ravi and Amelia to move from the doors, and Ba, Ma, Auntie Yee, and Uncle Yee were now in the hall. They were scanning the room, looking for Nai Nai and me. I crouched down, holding Nai Nai's shoulders.

"You can do it, Nai Nai!" I said.

Just then a man's voice screamed out. "House!"

It wasn't Nai Nai. I stood up to see who it was.

"Shut up, Barry, you're not even playing!" shouted Tommy over the microphone. "Keep those eyes down. Someone get Barry out! Maureen, we've told you before: he can come but only if he's quiet!" The unfortunate Barry was taken toward one of the fire exits. His mother got up and was still marking off her card as she walked backward.

Ma and Ba were now striding down the middle aisle, but instead of the frowns that I was expecting, they were both smiling. Ba put one arm around Ma as he walked toward us. I let go of my fears of being grounded forever. Ma pointed to Nai Nai, who was concentrating on the bingo screen, her eyes wide like a tarsier's.

Auntie Yee was jogging in her stilettos toward Amelia, who was standing like a deer in headlights, unable to move. Uncle Yee already had his hands up in a *Nothing to see here* manner.

"Danny is such a bad influence on Amelia. We've missed her audition because of you," Auntie Yee said, poking me in the shoulder. It was a pretty painful finger joust; those talons hurt.

My parents sped up to reach us. Ba put his hand out as if to say *STOP*. Ma calmly pulled me toward her out of Auntie

Yee's reach, then moved in front of me; she was finally going to stand up to Auntie Yee! I couldn't believe it. "Oh no, we don't go around poking other people's children, Clarissa; that is not okay. This is the last time you put my Danny down, so I suggest you find someone else to bully. And take up baking classes while you're at it . . . Your steamed cakes taste like rubber."

Auntie Yee was speechless—another first. She grabbed Amelia and marched her down the aisle to the exit. Uncle Yee was walking backward, bobbing his head in apology to Ma. I was so proud of my mom.

"Sorry, Su Lin, she's not been the same since that women's meeting. They judged her cake very harshly. I'll take them home. Apologies, apologies."

*Poor Uncle Yee,* I thought. But I was glad they were going.

"This is a ridiculous game!" shouted Auntie Yee, trying to get the last word in as always. She was met with a spatter of boos from the regulars. Enid and her cronies stood up menacingly and waved their fists at Auntie Yee as she stumbled out of the community center, declaring everyone in there a "heathen."

Amelia gave us a thumbs-up as she exited, her braces catching the light. She wasn't so bad after all. "This was awesome! Let's do it again!" she shouted.

I looked at my parents. "You're not angry?" I asked.

"Well, we found the note and we didn't know what to expect . . ." said Ma. "Or whether or not to be angry with you for not listening to us again. But seeing Nai Nai so happy, we can see why you wanted to bring her. She loves it here."

Ba was busy looking at the screen and then scanning Nai Nai's card.

Nai Nai was still waiting for number eight.

Ma put her arm around my shoulders and gave me a squeeze.

Ba grinned. He knew his mother was on the precipice of greatness. "Come on, Ma!" he squealed. I'd never seen my dad that excited before.

Nai Nai didn't move, except her ears might have twitched. She had two lychees stuffed into her cheeks. And then it happened. The number appeared on the screen. Eight.

Nai Nai rose and shouted, "Hao-si!!!" Number eight had saved the day.

She stood up on the table, waving her card—it was fully covered in lucky red dots. Nai Nai scrambled over the table and darted to the stairs, up to the stage, and toward Tommy. We all held our breath. You could cut the tension with a meat cleaver. I felt a finger joust in my side. Ravi was as nervous as I was.

Linda checked the numbers and then Tommy did a recheck using the screen to mark off the balls on Nai Nai's card. We watched as the numbers on the grid went black. Those were the ones Nai Nai had gotten.

*WINNER!!!* flashed in bright pink and yellow on the screen, and beneath: *£2000!!!!!*

We all communally exhaled.

"She's done it!" I exclaimed. My face was hurting from the size of my grin. Ravi and I started to jump around.

"She's won two thousand pounds?" Ba asked, looking up at his mother dancing on the stage. Ravi and I nodded. Ba kissed Ma on the cheek. "That's my mother! She's a winner!" he started to tell the bingo player nearest him, pointing up at Nai Nai. One old man even shook his hand. "That's MY MOTHER!" he shouted a bit louder.

"We know," came the deadpan reply of Enid's husband.

I looked up and Tommy was shaking Nai Nai's hand onstage. Nai Nai indicated that we should go up too. Without a second thought, Ba, Ma, Ravi, and I all ran up onto the stage and hugged Nai Nai. Our winner.

Linda was there too, holding a massive check. "I'm happy to announce, this lady, Nellie's friend, has won the jackpot! What's your name, love? I need to fill this bit in."

Nai Nai shouted "Hao-si" again. Ma and I laughed.

"Dong Mei! My mother's name is Dong Mei!" Ba cried out with glee. He spelled out the words for Linda, who wrote

Nai Nai's actual name on the giant check. "It means 'winter plums,'" he added.

I'd finally found out my grandmother's name and I couldn't think of one that would suit her better.

Tommy announced, "Dong Mei, also known as Winter Plums, has won this month's Grand Bingo Tournament! Do you have anything you want to say?" He held the microphone out to Nai Nai.

"Hao-si! Winner!" Nai Nai boomed into the microphone. The room erupted with marker pens being flung down onto tables in defeat. One lady started to clap and then more joined in. Even Enid's husband began clapping, but his wife slapped his hands.

Most of the room was cheering for Nai Nai. She was officially the best bingo player in the room. Nai Nai began kissing Tommy, the bingo caller, on the cheek. His face went the shade of a beet. Linda handed Nai Nai the giant check for two thousand pounds. Ma and Ba stood next to me with the biggest smiles I'd seen from them in ages. Nai Nai was on top of the world, holding up a check that was bigger than she was.

# CHAPTER 27

## MATH IS FUN!

**And to sum it all up, that was the day my nai nai from China won loads of money and changed the hearts of many people who weren't used to strangers.** She was the bravest person I'd ever met. I mean, she'd traveled thousands of miles to come live with us; she couldn't speak the language and didn't know anyone. She deserved more, especially from me. I made up my mind to really appreciate having her in my life. And she was a math champion, after all. I was really a lucky dragon, having her in my corner to help me with the one thing I wasn't good at.

We spent the second week of break working on my math project. I spent ages creating the most amazing illustrations to show how math could be found in nature and how

Fibonacci, a.k.a. Leonardo of Pisa, was a really cool dude for figuring that out.

Back at school on Monday morning, Mr. Heathfield pulled out people's names from a hat. The video camera was ready to record all of the presentations to be sent to the mayor's office, where the judging panel would choose the winner. The winning school would be notified once all of the videos had been sent in.

Carter's Fortnite presentation was a bit like watching lettuce wilt. I thought it would be exciting, but it was mostly him droning on about how many people he'd hit and how the probability of him beating his highest score was high.

Ravi's Hip-Hop Fractions was sooo awesome. He got the whole class swaying from side to side with their arms in the air. His cousin Deep came in with some turntables and flashing lights like you'd see at a disco. Ravi wore a knight's helmet and held a foil-covered shield that had loads of circles divided up into sections. There was a section for how many ogres he'd slain and how many maidens he'd rescued. I didn't even know Ravi could rap!

"Danny! Your turn," Mr. Heathfield said, giving me a thumbs-up. The red light flashed on the side of the camera.

"Yes, sir, a pleasure, sir." I was grinning. I'd never been so excited to talk about something math-related in my life. But to be honest, my topic didn't feel like it was math. It felt more like art.

I stood up in front of my class. My hands weren't sweating and I was breathing normally. "Everyone, I'd like to introduce you to my nai nai—Dong Mei." I said. "Her name means 'winter plums,' and I think that's why she loves fruit so much." I opened the door to the classroom, and Nai Nai came in carrying a basket of vegetables and fruit and my cardboard artwork.

"Today, my math presentation is about math in nature and art. A long time ago, a man called Leonardo of Pisa came up with the Fibonacci sequence . . ."

Nai Nai held up the large pieces of cardboard I had prepared. I'd drawn Leonardo with a long beard, a brown cloth dress, and a baseball cap. A speech bubble said: *I LOVE MATH, RIGHT ON!*

I got out the Romanesco cauliflower that Nai Nai had bought from Mr. Potempa's and passed it around the room. I heard oohing and aahing.

"Whoooaa! What IS THAT?" screeched Tia. I could see she was really impressed, for once.

"That's soooo freaky, but I like how it feels," said Grace as she ran her fingers over the green spikes. "So can you eat it?"

"What's this got to do with math?" Carter said, faking a yawn. I could tell he was jealous.

"Well, as some of you know, math is not my strongest subject. Despite that, my grandmother here showed me that math is all around. We don't need to be afraid of it. It's in nature, too."

Ravi gave me a little thumbs-up and a smile.

"I didn't know that," said Tia.

I went on to show them more sketches of Leonardo's sequence and how the numbers expanded and where you could find them in nature. Nai Nai had saved my butt. I could tell that even Mr. Heathfield was impressed.

He clapped his hands and actually patted me on the back after I'd taken a bow.

"Well done, Danny, and er . . . Danny's grandmother, who I am guessing did not draw these wonderful pictures," he said. "Thank you to those of you who presented today. You have blown me away. Both literally and otherwise . . ." Mr.

Heathfield looked over at Carter, probably remembering when Carter shot his Blaster gun during his presentation and hit Mr. Heathfield's bottom by accident. "And I can see you have worked hard on your presentations over the break. They were definitely entertaining and informative. We've filmed them all and will send them to the judges. We'll know by the end of the week who the regional prize winner is. If it's us, we'll tell you in the school assembly. Good luck, everyone. I'm really proud of you all."

Mr. Heathfield came over to me and leaned in. "I was really impressed with your drawings and how you thought outside the box, Danny. Keep up the good work. You know you can always come and ask me questions if you don't know how to do something, don't you?"

"Thank you, sir. I will," I told him.

I was sure someone like Amelia Yee would win, as she was always the best at everything. But even if I didn't win, I was happy to have created a great presentation for once. Nai Nai had shown me that actually Danny Chung DID do math, but in my own way.

On Wednesday after school, we took Nai Nai to see Mrs. Cruikshanks, who was still recovering in the hospital. When we told her that Nai Nai had won the Grand Bingo Prize, she whooped and cheered, pressing the orange button so she could tell the nurse on duty that her best friend had won the Grand Prize at bingo. The nurse fake smiled and told her the button was for emergencies and assistance only. Mrs. Cruikshanks started chanting "Hao-si! Hao-si! Hao-si!" and soon Nai Nai, Ba, and Ma were all doing it too. Ravi and I were trying to suppress our giggles when the staff nurse came and told us to be quiet.

Ba translated when Mrs. Cruikshanks said she was feeling much better and was lucky it wasn't a heart thing; it was a mini-stroke and she'd been told to get some rest for a few weeks.

"I don't know what I'm going to do if I can't go to bingo or do my charity work," Mrs. Cruikshanks said. "My house is too big just for me. That's why I like to be out and about. To see people and chat. How am I going to get my Chinese food if I'm stuck at home?"

"I can bring you the food," I told her.

"Ah, you're an angel, Danny," Mrs. Cruikshanks said. "And did you apologize to your nan here for those pictures you did?"

"I did. It's all fine now, and I even drew her a new comic where Nai Nai is a superhero."

"I'm glad." Mrs. Cruikshanks turned to Nai Nai and gave her a gummy smile. Her false teeth were in a plastic cup on the bedside table. "Dong Mei, such a lovely name," she said. "I wonder what she will spend her prize money on."

"Maybe it can help us buy a bigger house?" I asked Ba.

"Danny, Nai Nai would have to win quite a few of those Grand Prizes for us to buy our own place," Ba said.

"You'll have to keep sharing with her for a while yet," Ma added.

Mrs. Cruikshanks shifted a little upright. "I've just had a funny idea. I've got four spare rooms at my home. Two with bathrooms. My kids live in Santa Fe in America, so I never get visitors. Dong Mei can come stay with me if she likes. I've got a garden and you can come over and play anytime, Danny, with your friend here."

Ma looked at Ba, who looked at me. Then at Nai Nai. He translated the message from Mrs. Cruikshanks, and Nai Nai's face lit up. She practically beamed. She started babbling and then gave Mrs. Cruikshanks a big fat kiss.

"So that's sorted out, then!" said Mrs. Cruikshanks. "We'll be like *The Golden Girls* on the telly." I didn't know what she was talking about, but Ba laughed, and Ma chuckled too. Then Mrs. Cruikshanks started singing "Thank You for Being a Friend" while holding Nai Nai's hand.

Ba was the saddest of all to see Nai Nai move out, but Ma told him to stop crying.

"It's only five blocks away!"

Ba and Ma packed most of her things into the van and we pulled up outside Mrs. Cruikshanks's place—it was massive. Her husband had died totally unexpectedly, a bit like Ye Ye. No wonder she was out all the time; she was lonely in such a big house. Nai Nai walked up toward her new home at number 95 Birch Avenue with a smile on her face, carrying two massive laundry bags full of stuff. Mrs. Cruikshanks was standing by the front door, grinning wide. She was holding a banner that had been hastily scribbled with a bingo marker. It said: WEL-COME, NEW ROOMIE!

Finally the end of the week had come around. Friday was the big day—we were going to find out who had won the math presentation. The prize was spending a day with a limo and going to the Knights of Old theme park. My money was on Amelia or someone from her fancy school. We crowded into the main hall for the assembly—the whole school was there. Mr. Heathfield was onstage, which was unusual.

We all sat on the floor and looked up.

"Hello, school. Today we've been notified that one of our students has won the prize for the Math Is Fun presentation.

The winner will receive a day in a limo with friends, a meeting with the mayor of Birmingham, and tickets to the theme park Knights of Old."

"It's not going to be any of us," Carter said behind me.

Mr. Heathfield was smiling. "I'm more than proud to say that someone in my own class has won, and the limo is waiting outside as I speak."

The whole room oohed and aahed.

"Settle down," said Mrs. Brannan with force from the side of the hall.

Mr. Heathfield looked over toward me . . . "The winner is . . ." No way . . . was he going to say my name? Had Nai Nai's winning touch finally landed on me?

". . . Ravi Dalal from 6H for his Hip-Hop Fractions!"

Ravi looked at me, and I looked at him.

"Yes! Well done, Sir Rav!" I said excitedly. I hadn't come in first, but it didn't matter. I'd gotten to show that math wasn't always about doing calculations and I'd gotten to draw some awesome stuff too.

"Man! We're going to Knights of Old in a limo!" Ravi said. His grin was the biggest I had ever seen it.

"We?" I said, pretending that I didn't know he would totally be taking his best friend—who was me!

I gave him a double fist bump and then finger jousted him in the side. Mr. Heathfield waved his hand, urging Ravi to go up onstage to collect the tickets. As he walked, he looked just a little bit taller. His head was held high. He was Sir Ravi of Long-dale. Mighty rapper and slayer of fractions. The whole room clapped for him (apart from Carter, Mitchell, and Jay Jay, who had been arguing about whose fault it was that they hadn't won). It was the best week ever.

# EPILOGUE

## A Room of One's Own

**Ba and Ma took a few days off work, which had NEVER happened EVER.** They said that after seeing Nai Nai and me have so much fun together, they realized they had been missing out.

"We've been working too hard all these years, Danny, and Nai Nai has only been here a few weeks and understood what you like doing and who you are," said Ma.

"Yes, and I'm going to join a yoga class and take more time off work," said Ba. "My back pain was a sign that I was overdoing it."

My parents also said that I could have the room makeover I'd wanted for a long time.

They let me decide what colors to decorate my room. I chose a green called "verte," as it reminded me of the

Romanesco cauliflower. It was so much fun choosing how I wanted my room to look. I helped paint the walls and doors. Ma said I did a professional job, too.

She got me a new set of duvet covers that matched the walls. There was no more soccer duvet. Nai Nai had given Mrs. Cruikshanks the bobble hat, who wore it every time she went out. It went well with her grubby raincoat. And under my window, I had a new desk and chair with drawers for my paper and pens. In the corner was a beanbag and a TV mounted on the wall. I'd never have to leave my room again if I didn't want to!

The room was now ready for Ravi to come and have a sleepover, but the best part of all was that I had an ART WALL. I was pinning some of my drawings to it when Ma came in, announcing I had visitors.

"Nai Nai and Mrs. Cruikshanks are here with a new addition for your art wall," she said. Both women squeezed into my bedroom. Ma and Ba huddled near the window. Nai Nai handed me a large box that was covered in tissue paper from Mr. Potempa's. It had bananas printed on it. I ripped open the box, and there was one of Ye Ye's brush paintings of a dragon. I loved it. I felt a lump in my throat the size of a lychee and gave Nai Nai the biggest hug.

"Thanks, Nai Nai, I love it," I said.

Ba came over and hung it up on a hook that I hadn't noticed before, and straightened it. Then he started wiping his eyes. "Something in my eye, just some dust." He turned away.

Ma came over then and put her arms around me. "We love you, Danny, and we want you to know that, with or without a fancy room."

"Thank you, both of you," I said. "It's perfect."

We stood in a row and looked at my new wall of awesomeness. It had my best sketches—the Druckon, Stunt Snail, Ant Gran, Superhero, and on the right, my math presentation certificate. It said my presentation was "highly commended." Ba had pinned up my drawing of Leonardo of Pisa, who I discovered did some other cool stuff along with the Fibonacci sequence, like helping to popularize the numbers we use today instead of Roman numerals. Math would be extra hard if we all had to use Roman numerals, that was for sure.

"Thank Nai Nai," Ba said. "She insisted she wanted to pay for lots of this new stuff."

"But I thought you hated art because it had no purpose," I said to Ba.

"I was wrong. Ye Ye was an artist, just like you. And he gave up a very good job to pursue his art. I blamed him because we didn't have enough money for me to attend college. I came here instead, and we never forgave each other. To me art didn't have a purpose; it only brought us sadness." Ba pulled me close and hugged me. "I'm sorry, Danny . . . for stopping you from drawing. It's your gift; I see that now."

Nai Nai tapped me on the arm, then handed me something long rolled up in a paper towel. I peeled it open and inside were some wooden paintbrushes.

"They were your ye ye's," Ba said. Ba pulled out some blank canvases from behind the door. "Here, Danny, we want you to do what makes your heart sing," he said. "Draw, paint, and whatever you do will make us proud."

I couldn't believe it. No more Chinese Way lectures, no more talks about everything having to have a purpose, no more wanting me to be more like Amelia. I rushed over and gave my dad the biggest hug. Then everyone else piled on for a group hug.

"This is so emotional," said Mrs. Cruikshanks, wiping her eyes.

"Thank you," I said, holding up the paintbrushes.

I put my arms around Nai Nai. She patted my back.

"I love you, Nai Nai," I said.

"Hao-si," she replied.

# ACKNOWLEDGMENTS

Thank you, José, for being supportive when I've gone away to write and for believing in my dream. My two children, Santiago and Alma, thank you for letting me "borrow" small snippets of your lives for my writing and for being very honest beta readers. You are both awesome and I love you so much.

Thank you to my agent, Chloe Seager, for being a bright star and for calling me up to tell me I was going to be a debut author! Thank you to the staff at Madeleine Milburn Literary, TV and Film Agency for your hard work. I'd like to thank Alice Sutherland-Hawes for signing me as a new author and for championing the idea that became this novel.

My editors at Abrams Kids, Erica Finkel and Emily Daluga, thank you both for bringing Danny Chung to U.S. readers! I have enjoyed working with you both. Thanks to my U.K. editor, Georgia Murray, and the team at Piccadilly Press for seeing something in my writing. Editors are amazing beings! And my novel is more nuanced and better for all of your input. Thanks to those behind the scenes too.

Thank you to Natelle Quek for providing such vibrant and humorous illustrations. I was a big fan before we began working together, and now I am an even bigger fan! Check out Natelle's work here: natellequek.com

And thanks to you the reader! My university major was in American Studies and I spent some time living in the Bay Area, so I am so thrilled that U.S. readers will get to meet Danny Chung and his family.